I0531623

Storylandia

The Wapshott Journal of Fiction

Issue 18

The Wapshott Press

Storylandia, Issue 18, The Wapshott Journal of Fiction, ISSN 1947-5349, ISBN 978-1-942007-07-4, is published at intervals by the Wapshott Press, PO Box 31513, Los Angeles, California, 90031-0513. All correspondence can be sent The Wapshott Press, PO Box 31513, LA CA 90031-0513. Visit our website at www.WapshottPress.com This work is copyright © 2016 by Storylandia. The Wapshott Journal of Fiction, Los Angeles, California. Copyright © 2016 Thomas Hrycyk and is reprinted here with the copyright owner's permission.

Storylandia is always seeking quality original short stories, novelettes, and novellas. Please have a look at our submission guidelines at www.Storylandia.WapshottPress.com or email the editor at editor@wapshottpress.com

Cover: "The Night You Slept," by Cinthya Espitia. www.farbstiftebox.tumblr.com

Storylandia

The Wapshott Journal of Fiction

Founded in 2009

Issue 18, Spring 2016

Edited by Ginger Mayerson

Table of Contents

L'Amande et la Fleur

by

Thomas Hrycyk

L'Amande et la Fleur

"See the orient dew?" the Japanese soldier asked. "See how it sheds from the bosom of the morning." The old man called it *Sennin*. He told me it was Chinese and adopted in love. He also believed it was part of the spirits of nature—or of the air—to him it was all the same. The old soldier's front tooth was missing and the other was covered in a sort of pink molasses. He pulled out paper and sat down on the rock in front of me. He placed some heroin in the paper, licked his lips, and rolled it up setting the cigarette in his mouth and tilting it upward at a 45 degree angle. The heroin, having been packed too tightly, puffed out on his exhale as brown snow between us. He stared at me with one good eye, taking in shallow breaths. I think he was on the lookout and convinced the war wouldn't end until his own eye bore it. From then on, I understood little else about him. He said he came up from the village just down the mountain, though he evidently was lost and had reached the age where he should have been thinking of his next incarnation. He began to talk up the sato-wood as he took it from his bag and peeled its skin, stuffing the upper part of his boots with it. "I came from Chang Kan, go that way," his arms flailed in an eastern direction as he spoke. "Spicy bushes burn better there. Find the fence. Near the river. Near the mountains. Only so many ways there." He strolled off mumbling. "*O ma ni pa dme hum.*"

"What does that mean?" I asked.

He hadn't the faintest idea. The old man limped along, trying to forget all that happened before him. He scooped up pebbles near the edge of the trail and hurled them into the brush as if to scare away some demons.

I met another Japanese soldier up near Huzhou, said he came up somewhere between Kamakura and Enoshima. He took all his belongings and was throwing them into a pile. There were women sitting at the stream pounding clothes on rocks. He kept piling up his possessions and eventually removed his clothing. Behind him was Yixing with ugly blotches of villages in the hills and slums where nature should have been left alone. Even from the river you could hear the terrified squeal of a pig throughout the night and it found ways to keep you awake. The soldier wasn't even sure of himself as he spoke, washing in the shallow stream that pushed up against his ankles. He told me he visited a man who spoke many tongues and was described only as *fulvous hue'd* and *whistling*. He had information on his missing wife. "You know what they say here?" he asked, pushing water up to his armpits. "They call you *Pyigling pa.*"

"What's that?"

"*Inconnu.*"

"Oh."

"I couldn't."

"Couldn't?"

"Take their heads or their children."

As the day moved on, it became mist-wreathed in its best face. The normal filth was washed off by the vaporous spritz of moonlight. My nights—usually spent slumbered on the shores of Beihai or Chang Fei Sha where the waters of the Sea laugh up at you—were far behind me now. The mountain landscape in front of me swam in blue. I walked along the trickling creek, hundreds of miles from soldiers, from sounds, and from Time and its racking. Behind me was the godly work of Yeou. In front of me was so much more. Up all the inclines and slopes and steep climbs, I eventually found my way to a flat plateau. I discovered an open-spaced wattle and daub shack with loose slats in its framing. There were stones and mud in a crude design with crooked lines and strange tiny windows peeking through. There was a rough wooden framework with a wooden partition down the center, the windows looked to have slanted eyebrows above them. For as high up as it was, it was well kept and preserved. It appeared to be built in a hurry but that in no way subtracted from its structural integrity.

After miles of travel, the fatigue disease was on me, and this was the best time to cease and desist. I approached the shack hoping to find someone friendly inside. There was no door, only a fur tarp on the entrance, dewed in the mist.

"The rose colored sphinxes, those came from the 1867 Exposition. I myself am more interested in the early gothic antiques I keep in my private stables," she grabbed my arm tightly and pulled me out onto the patio and into the yard as she continued speaking. "Gobelins tapestries, Japanese frames, Breton furniture, carved figurines, it is my own collection. But what I see as interesting you, my dear, is you take a look at the library of over 10,000 books. There I keep priceless documents pertaining to the French Revolution, facsimiles

of their true origin and color, rare books by Baudelaire Verhaeren and Gide, and every book on artwork that ever existed before and during this century." Phèdre de Belzunce laughed. We made our way back into the château. "Father hides his collection of ancient firearms and weapons. Mother never let him keep them out on the display; that right is for Mother and her Beauvais tapestries. They're much more pleasant on the eyes." Phèdre stopped in the hallway taking both of my hands into hers. She twirled in a circle and swayed around me. We danced for what seemed like hours. Her warm hands embraced as equally as the whole—her body into mine. Her footwork was light and magnificent. "There is more to see but you must be tired. How much did you sleep?" she asked. The questions continued one after the other. *Was there much at the orphanage to do? Did you read a lot? I bet you read a lot. Painters read a lot, I hear. Have you met other artists? Did you always work alone? What inspires you? Did you sleep a lot?* etc., etc., *ad* almost *infinitum.*

I stared quizzically *en revanche.* I was never much of a talker. Plus, she had swept me away with her hospitality and beauty.

"You can sleep here, my lovely Jules, but not too late, for tomorrow is Christmas," her eyes lit up as she spoke. "The night before has certainly lent itself to being perfect wouldn't you agree?"

I nodded.

"After the star found our Saviour, it was supposed to find a nail and hang itself up in our corner of the universe. This was our era of splendor. Its divine mission wasn't over though for it was handed its sublimity too early. Why are the predecessors to Christ to be forgotten? That is why I set out the most royal and holy of monstrances to illuminate with might and good power. Though it had no idea what I value, I sent it on its way across the globe. It's on the chalets, glory be to God, they tell me that stars shine on laughing countries, the ones which by the night of penetrating perfumes, chrysanthemums that blossom at the base of these mountains, waking the herdsmen and hunters alike, it will provide an illuminating force for laboring. The red velvet fur of the smaller panda and the flowers bursting forth — it departs for the peonies which always watch the heavens and are happy for whoever keeps them as their charms." Phèdre laughed again as we made our way to the dining room. She sat down with a pillowy *umph*. It had been close to midnight and I had not slept all of the night before. I had been far too anxious to move out of the orphanage and everything in the moment had seemed far too surreal.

"I cannot go a long way," I told her. "Sleep comes soon."

"You mustn't bed yet, this young evening is far from over." Phèdre clapped her hands together. "The radio of Cavalleria Rusticana is downstairs. We can spread out on velvets on our stomachs and listen, yes?"

"Will the hour after midnight dismiss me?"

"Yes," she responded. "Everything past it is yours."

The Christian midnight is a solemn time as of yore. For it was midnight which repaired what was wrong and the Imperial Magi and the sailing of Maries to Oppidum-Ra which corrected that which needed it. Christmas midnight, Iczot Hallelal...

I began to drift off as the radio played. I ended up somewhere between the two worlds. I found myself in a nightmare of heavy curtains, dreaming only of all the ruin I was about to cause in this poor girl's world. There are people, and people of varying depths and intricacies of character, none that compare with my own, who are so much more deserving to be occupying this scene of paintings of old ancestors I am unable to appreciate. I awoke from my state and picked myself up. This was a difficult task, seeing as how my soon-to-be-wife was draped over me in heavy slumber. Her breaths were so shallow, I checked a few times to make sure her heart still beat in its chamber. I made my way to the bedroom. Beyond the double-wide bay window with its ruby blinds half-drawn, as far out as I could see, the suburbs of Paris were wrapped in the smoke of slums and warehouse factories. Out there, all those beasts of burden like me, with their ugliness and appetites for more—thinking they can get the most out of life—thinking they drew the number no one else could. A heavy snowfall blanketed the streets of Paris.

I walked onward. The dining room looked like an untouchable crypt with drawings in sanguine by Boucher and Watteau and *St Vincent Taking the Place of Two Galley Slaves* by Leon Bonnat. The nudes by Puvis de Chavannes in the den struck me as being more blown-out-looking-things comparatively. There was a large botanical table whose lilac breche marble sloped top reflected itself on the beach glass, surrounded by candelabrums from Tiffany and Company. The remains of dinner, four sweets, were placed on the table facing away from one another. Rhubarb pies, apple tarts, strawberries with Devonshire cream, and trembling jellies— the color and transparency of amber. One gathers that the master chef would walk about the house with his thumb permanently stuck in old cookery books or in a Dumas gastronomic dictionary. He did haunt the kitchen in most hours, even in the middle of the night. He was usually found weeping tears of blood over failed concoctions. He was one of true ambrosia and sweat.

The château seemed incredibly well-run and polished as if to reflect in on itself, all of its light, airy, speckless six acres of well-designed grounds. The garden outside was shaped to Le Nôtre's taste with Cedars and Japanese copper beeches carefully planted. Some of the trees' trunk measurements were over six metres. I made my way through the reception room which was seven and a quarter metres high, filled with daguerreotypes, crates of Japanese porcelain figurines, locked cabinets, and a jumbled array of unusual furniture. The walls had been hung with mezzotints of cathedrals and ancient churches along with being covered in cryptic maxims: *Absentes absunt* over the entrances and *A diabolo qui est simian dei* on the back of the chairs. All the rooms seemed so full of memories for Phèdre and her family. I found my way into the bedroom and slept.

The next morning, I awoke and made my

way downstairs. Some cats marched across the Persian rugs as no one cared to observe. On a lacquered table incrusted with Mother of pearl, there resting on a grinning negro-held frame was a photograph of Phèdre and her family. I picked it up and took a gander. I had rarely seen a photograph in my life. It had nearly brought me to tears.

The gifts were now being brought out by the servants, each handled so delicately. The way the Belzunces looked out into the hallway waiting for the next servant to tiptoe into the chambers, you would have believed that Proteus had metamorphosed into a cabochon ruby clip, able to give the future. The next few minutes were quiet like tombstones until Monsieur de Belzunce chimed in as often as he does.

Phèdre's father was the embodiment of quixotic nobility. He was incredibly thin and tall. He looked cadaverous in nature with deeply sunken, glaucous eyes, fleshless lips, and dark beady pupils that seemed to have sped toward you like raging bullets. As usual, he was inordinately preoccupied by his ancestry. He managed nevertheless to coax a procession of dead kings from his sometimes scattered memory. "It has been said that I have a cultivated taste for a princely past. They have called me Simon Zelotes. I prefer to be known as a genealogical zealot, it is a more fervent accuracy."

"Are you well-versed in Antoine Phillipe de la Trémoïlle?" I asked.

"If he ever lost a pearl of sweat, I hunted the Earth for it." Although Monsieur de Belzunce was no longer at the forefront of political debates as he once had been, his uncanny sense of augury still seemed in full force. He had written to the Republic about the inevitable conflict with Germany—one that closely resembled that of 1870. Monsieur looked up at the ceiling. "Not too long ago, clever and evil men somehow persuaded the French that they could liberate themselves by chopping off the head of their king. By listening to this pernicious advice, the people found a way to decapitate themselves." Phèdre's parents had still been stuck on figures like Scheurer-Kestner saying things like, *He was a valet of German ideals, he was utterly the gray eminence of treason and disgust — slime that had to be washed out into the sewers never to return.*

They continued to open gifts. I had been too new to the family and therefore there was nothing for me. Phèdre had found me at Campden Hills Home for Boys, she asked for the man who was responsible for painting *L'Amande et la fleur*. She came to me in my room, there were twin bedsteads of pure white, two washstands, and on my wall, drawings and prints of my efforts. I had to sell my paintings and give the profits to the orphanage to stay. In doing so successfully, they let me commandeer my own room. Phèdre came to me one evening and told me she would help me leave Campden Hills, she only needed a few days for paperwork. She saw something in me that no one else did, not even myself. Though *L'Amande et la fleur* was certainly my most difficult work, it meant nothing special to me, like a deformed child I was to rid myself of. Before she returned, I accustomed myself to the big winter garden nearby, the only one in the VIIth arrondissement of Paris. It was two weeks until Christmas and she found me sleeping outside, when she came and took me away.

Phèdre had just exchanged a lover's gift with her mother, a Fabergé egg in a necklace adorned with amorous devices, it was Gatchina Palace crushed on her chest. Phèdre shot up in excitement. "Let us remember this as the first Christmas of the Magi, of Melchoir, of Jules!" she shouted. "It is proclaimed, this would all be more authentic if we owned scholarly rights and dressed in Pirahan costume!"

I stood up. "The burden of bringing me into this household is gift enough," I said. "Thank you everyone." I took a seat again and thought back on my past holidays. Christmas found ruined fortune in earlier years for me. I asked Jesus questions every year on his birth. *What if this was the world's last night?* My mind on those dreary, damp, cold nights did whet to seek out God. But now, my mind was occupied and temporarily content. Was this love?

Inside the shack was the voice of a man curling in on itself. The clang of metal struck in on the corners of sound over the singing in deep slave tones. "Hey nonny, nonny no. Sigh no mo, ladies. Sigh no mo." The man sang with miraculous organ as he belted onward. I saw his honey-red skin through the fettered hairs of the lining. There was about four inches between the wooden frame and the tarp. "Hey nonny nonny, nonny no."

I approached slowly. I asked with a whisper if he spoke French. He didn't, but I knew more than enough English to be comfortable in conversation.

"Wonderin' like a loss dog?"

"Yes," I said to the man.

"You not wonna those parlor pinks?" He was chipping wood with a hatchet, turning his head back to his work every time he spoke up.

"No, sir."

"A man of true bonhomie," he said smiling. His dark skin was slick, sweaty, and the color of a cherry wood burnt in hell's fires. His feet were dusty, full of splinters and he could have been chipping at that log for hours now. He stood next to a stove in the center of the room. The stove was sloppily in the shape of a square with holes in the corners. There was mud built up in three corners to support the cooking pots. These were made of copper. I wondered whether the man had tinned them himself.

"Are you familiar with France?" I asked.

He shook his head, but he changed his mind and began to nod. "Fairy France—Unitarded—Ephemy real—Emanciparticipation."

"Have you heard of me then?"

"You must be the findness fancyman in all of France," he sung it to me like a verse. His voice quickly settled in. "I'm sure you think I know your story but what a useful crutch that would be!"

He could tell I didn't want that question to come out. He saw my eyes. He saw what I wanted. He turned back to his work. I took a step forward. He pulled the tarp to the side and told me his name was Solly and that he was from Alabama. He gently strode to the side and stepped out from his work. I looked at the stream dipping off the mountain walls. It was louder than my voice. I found myself speaking up during conversation. The water fell off the mountain like lead, as if it were chained to a phaéton.

The firs were bending like a wax candle left to the noon. The leaf-covered lanes were all a-tremble with men in smart ties and bowler hats, chimneysweeps with unkempt mustaches and calloused hands and women in colorful skirts and crisply starched shirts crowded the way. Before I met Phèdre, I found most of life's pleasures outside the orphanage between the boulevards somewhere off in the distance of Madeleine's and Tortoni's. A favorite pastime—taking a stroll down the boulevards watching the children running wild and conquering the carrousel. *Tournez tournez bons chevaux de bois.* I sat on the benches before a weather-torn proscenium. I watched as the laudaus swept by, swaying in a ceaseless stream of fiacres, coupes, and victorias. A cacophony of hoofbeats had me wondered-eyed as the pebbles spurted under the carriage in the cluttered thunder of the Imperiale. The way the horses threw their heads down—neighing in a constant vocal flutter—I almost expected to see Adrastus in one of those creaking beasts.

I lost myself until children zoomed by, trodding on my toes. I truly did live the life of a flâneur, for no cares would be had, except for flavoring the gourmet city. The florid faces looking through mesh—those carriages getting damnably hot in the afternoon with the sun riding the roofs. My brothers and I used to call them Phlegethons as we imagined the percherons were bred in hell's fires, taking flesh as food. Sometimes we found a top hat blowing away, past the Société Genéralé near the Au Printemps, with bodyguards serving as entertainment.

An annoyed man followed the hat in gallop as we laughed deeply at him. He moved past the hunchbacks carrying brand new jewels and the barrels with which to honor Shamshi. I always took notice of the old clock surveying the building wall, time itself and its role as past and inheritor. My brothers and I found a sable cloak in an alleyway and checked the pockets as a lady late for a fitting at Callot Soeurs walked by. All the ladies with beauty were clad as a cavalcade of show-buggies refurbished with plumes and fleur-de-lis'd banners and hitched to three pairs of prancing grays with buckled shoes, feathered boas, and made up faces. The footmen were decked in gold-embroidered liveries and near them, the wind hit the dahlias of the garden, making them undulate in purple sways and flash onto golden canes spangled in the sunlight. The cicadas hummed like disease and quinine. The owl-like smuttings of women in the cafés with their candy-box looks tore through the town. A tiny black heel wearing a white cotton stocking peeping out, sending men into flourishing.

"Of course I'm your friend. I'm their friend and I'm everybody's friend. That's the spirit here, the Parisienne spirit. Well, except for Madame, and what she had done. No spirit can resuscitate that." The lady at the table was chewing her food softly as she spoke.

"Agreed," the other woman responded. "She turned him to the worst. He once was an easygoing man of the world. Now—well—now he is a boorish lout. Maybe in time she will conceal the nature of her amorous leanings."

"His luminous spirit once was enough to

give one the day itself."

On their table were half-eaten cream puffs and champagne that cost four francs a bottle. That was gone now. They both had intentions to visit Jacques Goudstikker after their meal. The one woman's foot was dancing underneath the table in anxiety.

"I'm looking for more of a chrysophrase color on my collar. I'll even settle for a porphyry or malachite if I can get the dagging tailored on at the last moment by Paul."

"You go to Poiret's down there also?" she asked.

The other lady scoffed. "When you're going to a wedding like this, you show up in a debonair carriage drawn on by high steppers with red poppy flowers in their bridles and when you step down, your dress and ambiance best be attributed to a wholly Parisian refinement to your appearance. On another note, Italian hints may be acceptable."

"Splendid," the second woman shot up, shaking the table. "I've decided on an Italian tailor, a dress of pearl pink."

"An instant classic I'm sure."

The women paid and left the café with parasols with flounces and frillings in hand. A copy of *Le Gaulois* fluttered its way from under the glass vase and into the city's artery.

I sauntered down the anamorphic boulevard that kept on changing its mind from *Louis Marin* to *rue de l'Abbé de l'épée* to *rue Henri Barbusse* to *rue de l'Est* to *rue de la Harpe*. There isn't much prettier than an audience of young matrons at an evening concert. Oh, these women claim to be out for air, but are also there to make the world aware of their perfect existence. That much I did know. Valet de pieds held their gloved hands and gently clouded them off their cabriolet while the white mules (which were special gifts) with bridle chains of sterling silver brayed off into the dusk. The verdure was in bloom. The gardens were fresh and new.

The pink of the city was exiting, it was becoming difficult to see that the sun had already blistered the paint on the church walls and it all soon became gold. Some men would have hair as wet as Bois de Boulogne at night as they sometimes dunked their heads in water at salons to clear their minds for fresh and riveting ideas. The anti-Semitics born of the Dreyfus era stalked the wisteria and honeysuckle hedges after a brief dinner, trying to sneak a peek on the newest and freshest girls coming from the salons, judging first their snouts even before passing critique on their fat and bespectacled appearances. The omnibus, having practically fallen off the circus-ring roadways, made way for the open landaus, broughams, and night horses orchestrated by cochers with tiers of capes and a sense of duty similar to the dray horses standing and twitching their ears. The cochers flicked flies off them. The spectacle of useless but blithe humans combing horses and pretty taffetas that puts everyone in the spirit.

Tonight was darker than normal, even the Orléanists were nowhere to be seen. Bald men with cudgel fighting sticks strolled down the avenues between the storefronts and broke from the alleys when there were no lights provided.

Even in the night, the church which usually seemed robust and full of hungry souls had been gearing itself up for the largest wedding France had seen in years. And that wedding was my own.

The boulevard no longer smelt of bad cheeses as the moon fell upon the hedges of Père Lachaise like a pale page from the Bible, clad in the sable vestre of the dead and demons. The tall chimneys looked like campanili and the houses like palaces. The whole place hung itself in the corner of Heaven as its personal fairyland. I wondered once fame struck me deeply, if this would be the last trip here of anonymity I would enjoy. I asked myself this, returning back to my fiancée in the night.

Solly took a seat on the loadstones outside. He looked worn down, but excited to see another human being who knew some English. The questions came on again *ad* almost *infinitum*—one after another. *Where were you born? Who molded you? Carpeaux? Where is the camp of Maurica? Where is the river of Calonne? How does one forticate? Where does the English Channel end? Where does Normandy begin? Who is William the Bastard?* I answered each question as quickly as I could. "I've givin' too much to talk 'bout. Where my manners? W'y don you come on in and eat something with me?"

"I couldn't," I said in all honesty. "I should be on my way."

The rejection was immediate and none too soon. "Rest, for a moment at least. My wet gaze on this wearied face stamped with majesty looks worn. This firmament studded with stars and sun and Heaven is mirrored in those eyes and currently dulled out." Solly was busy scrapping away at some moss as he looked desperately at me like a poor puppy.

"I do love a good chat, but I live for adventure." I was lying as he cut me off.

"Fatal glaciers, hard-slabbed climbs, you will have to go a long way round if you wanna avoid 'em. Especially besmirched within a belly's full wailin' and night's demise. I got meat, I got veggies, an fruit—it's a devil of a fix," Solly snapped his wrist in my direction and laughed. "Jezcri, you ought to see all the warm bodies I got comin' my way and leavin' for the better."

"Sure," I chirped. "I'll stay *but* a brief moment," I emphasized.

He chuckled in victory. "All flesh is clay with fruitful changes, no reason to be frosty." He stood and motioned his chiseled arm as if attempting to wring acorns from lilies. In celebratory fashion, he took me by the fingertips and pulled me toward the shack. I ducked past the tarp. The smell of woods was peaceful inside, saturated with mountain ozone and the perfume of wild mint and parsley. I was expecting more of a mess than I saw. There was saffron, cumin, ginseng, wolfberries, dang gui, and rhubarb hanging from the branches and jars fermenting in a clear color.

I was curious. "What are those?" I lifted my hand and groped around for a jar.

"Brandy," Solly said, sending me a wink.

My brothers called it Sacre Chien. They would say, we speak loudly now but the wine will Silenus. Brandy, *my other brother would correct him,* it's brandy, not wine.

The younger sisters in the front bedrooms had thrown off their quilts and lay under transparent sheets where the presence of them was revealed. The night was hot, rather sticky and steamy even as the wind curled the oval clothes weighed down by trinkets on the drawers. Phèdre's sisters were fast asleep, profoundly unconscious within seconds. Choucroute garnie was bubbling away in the kitchen with aromas filling the stairs and the rooms.

There were nights to be had and women dreaming of luring me into their scented boudoirs. I had heard of a required sense of sowing oats from the gentlemen around me. The need for a mistress, they discussed it openly though they said you must never divorce—never. A mistress was acceptable they told me this. This night had been unlike anything I had ever experienced before. I paint a picture of untrammeled revel.

Phèdre had three sisters, Mademoiselles Clara, Juliette, and Lozana, courtesans whose flawless beauty was once the toast of three continents. They sowed their wild oats far more often than Phèdre had ever desired. They believed there would always be a wanting in life like dead branches that never grew leaves. And the Belzunces worried about the wild behavior of Phèdre's oldest sister Lozana, who always seemed entirely out of control with her drinking and her men. She jumped from one bed to the next with such careless abandon that the elder Belzunces feared it would bring her to a tragic end along with her two other sisters. Most assumed she would be felled by a jealous wife perhaps if she continued to be unsafe in her sowings. They assumed that the three sisters were most closely related to their aunt, a well-known insane person—the unsettling genealogy had its own point to prove.

Lozana's tongue was in my ear as I lay in my chamber. "Let's go down into the basement, there she won't be able to see us and let's drink of this rinquinquin of joie and enjoux," she whispered in my ear, her breath already putrid from drink. "And beware of the great Tarasque and enjoux because underneath the stairs are short legs, ribbed and swelled, and scorpion stings and in the wood of le boeuf et l'ours et venin profonde." Lozana began to move her hand lightly over my chest, stimulating the hairs one by one. "My ill need of hairy whooze and all the heirlooms the size of pinpricks and you, the beginning to kingdoms—you've come to loose madness on me," she whispered, pulling my hand and getting me up from bed.

Other ladies joined us as we made our way down. There was Mademoiselle Juliette of great beauty, Mademoiselle Clara of celestial beauty, Madame Lozana claiming to have escaped Heaven itself and bringing two angels, Madame Francine and Mademoiselle Violet with her; they were virgins of Brioude and Kaysersberg. So we went down to the basement and I saw the room full of palm-wood casks and we drank, without touching our lips to the spout and got drunk and they took off all their clothes because they said an orgy was to take place. Wine was running down their legs and they sang, *Tout en chantant sur le mode mineur. L'amour vainqueur et le vie opportune. Ils n'ont pas l'air de croire à leur. Bonheur et Leur chanson se mêle au clair de lune.* And everyone danced together pell-mell, the women with the women and man with man, all were sopping and dripping down their legs. The Mmes hadn't changed, they were still beautiful with liquids knitted to their legs. They climbed upon the casks and rode them and danced the Waltz of the Toreaders upon them. They were all enticing and tempting—hips flowing like undulous waves and falling like breasts and knees on casks. The surge of waists and fleshy buttocks—stomachs protruding and caving in—underwear clinging and wet—cheeks hollowed out and filling in— underwear foaming, frothing out—shoes falling out and revealing tiny toes and dresses slipping down from the animal which they were stripped.

"You must be an Andalusian beauty," it was Lozana speaking. "All would come to marry you. Come climb up the casks."

"Woman, you've made mankind a martyr," I replied.

She grabbed my finger tips and pulled me up onto the caskets, the grain of wood was like perfume. I pulled in her hips in front of me. She turned to offer me the corners of her mouth like a pot of rose marguerites and a spasm of pleasure seized me when I thought in these acute moments about the buoyant vitality and shining health of those fine young bodies that are feminine down to the fiber of their being. My sensitive nerves were reeking and swimming in sensuality like a drunken Bonaparte. The pads of my feet were dangling off until Lozana clasped my calves, lifted them upward and spread me on the pinewood. She wriggled her way onto me until her legs were dangling perpendicular to my hips as she squirmed with all her limp extremities and posthumous phony profundities.

Phèdre was in the hallway as her sisters crawled their way up the stairs with clothes falling off, fettered and falling down, sprawled along the solemn staircase. I saw the Nigerian maid talking with Phèdre as I attempted to sneak by:

"The sisters demanded girls and women in on my name and they led these people to the men's bedrooms and bathrooms because your sisters take things by force," the maid was close to tears as she confessed. "Your Grace, look upon the women yourself, but quietly, without letting them know you are there. They were in the basement a moment ago. They sometimes hide in the men's bedrooms and I have refused them a meeting nor were I with them in the basement. They were never to see me at night, they only share an upstairs vacancy with me. Such rotten, terrible impudence, they put me together with gesticulating prisoners of whom I always attempt to refuse their company."

The maid was out of breath and could not continue speaking. Phèdre's understanding was like her face, full of mannerisms but elegant withal. We understand dalliance here in France, but hardly take notes on it. I was able to sneak by without her noticing.

"Ghest in the household, ghest in the household, ghest in the household," Solly looked like a preacher as he pronounced each syllable with such exaggeration. He wore a rag as a shirt with roughly sewn patches applied at every angle, as true to God as he was to himself. "Mama said that errtime we crawled in our pajamas into the kitchen. She always been there, in that kitchen, seeing us through the back of her eyes. *Ghest in household, ghest in household, come in ghest, new and shiny. Come into my house, but you still young and can wait. Ghests aren't allowed in the kitchen, especially chillen.*" Solly handed me a plate of smoked meat. It was seasoned with an assortment of spices. It had heat and somewhat of a maple flavor to it.

"It's Mama Garçon's special recipe, five alarum," Solly was licking his fingers while he spoke. "Mama Garçon's heart turned to fat. And all that re-tart fat."

"I'm sorry," I said with a mouthful. I could only assume she had to be fairly young the way he looked at the plate while he savored each bite. He gnawed it and sucked on it until it dissolved in his mouth. His face was how I imagined Dionysos in each and every moment.

He was back to licking his fingers and staring deeply into them. He could have been talking to himself for all I knew. "You know what Mama used to tell me when I cried or complained 'bout my healf? She said, *You still have ya teef of pearl and yo coral colla nails. What mo you need?*"

I asked Solly if he wanted to speak of something else. He looked relieved. There was silence between us for a moment. But it was comforting. The rinds of the camphor overpowered the thin air. "I thank you much for the food, sir," I said.

"You're very polite. Hard to find that in people w'en errthin' suckt up from slime." Solly threw some ayug dry root into a pile, he was planning on making a fire.

They were talking about me in the other room as I stood in a Christ pose. My arms were getting heavy as a tailor measured out my sizes. I could hear all the others in the adjacent room.

"He is unworldly," said a man's voice. "There are no airs here and it's a little frightening. If he wants to get on with the world he better quickly find his tongue. He's faster to search for the answers to problems before finding his words."

An echo in the hallway responded in a deep, guttural voice. "He has more than a smattering of education which is good, but to acquire elegant manners is the next step. He needs also to be skillful at conversation and a sense of timing. He is an omnivorous reader and a genuine scholar at heart."

"What else?" A whiny man's voice screeched.

"He is a philoger."

"He is also a fervent spectator of the efforts of other people," a woman chimed in.

"I have plenty of work to do," the whiny man said. "They say the observer is the one who usually was the victim of action."

There was a time—a year or two since I had always been a sensitive boy—I was a stupid boy at that. I used to be struck deep for it too. Young boys were too unkind to me with unfriendly ridicule. *Eighteen and eighteen is what?* the teacher would ask. I didn't know, and I was struck deep for it. It affected everything. My handwriting became wavering, more so than a marbled fish steak fresh off the serpent. Painting only further destroyed my esteem. In autumn time, the bigger kids would tie me to a tress with thin string and when you struggled, it cut into your skin and sometimes they tied you up and threw you into wheelbarrows. The dormitories at twilight, the deathly anxieties of being called to the chalkboard to be interrogated by cruel teachers, attempts to cheat off fellow classmates, protected by book walls, a flood of physical abuse, cold sweats through the night with a ruckus tied up in the strings and heart. All my memories of the orphanage begin where the classroom lets out. The playground attributes to the cold sweats I so often felt as a child, if it were not that, it was the blackboard's chopping block. My life was scuffles, pranks, and victimizing — these are all the memories of a dunce, a bad pupil, and a soon-to-be freed man. I still remember the snowballs and streams of blood I spit up yearly. The snowball usually contained a rock in its center. The odor of dirty bare feet and carbolic acid that wafted up from the un-swept floors to mix with the heat and the flies and the chemical fumes coming from the room with all the sick children.

"Why if I'd ever marry him, I'd have to crack open his head for fear that his large brain is creating far too much pressure on his cranium," the woman's voice whispered. "Genius is always a terror to itself and to its epoch."

"That brain is eminently fitted for philosophic speculation and not much more in tense moments. An education must be given him and I shall entertain myself in giving it." The voice was that of Mme Gauthier. I was learning the art of imitating her bourgeois speech, she who talked about everything and who didn't like to be supplanted by a handsomer woman of lower birth who pointed out all the mistakes of the grisette. She incurred her hatred and the new favorite subject took care to keep her away from talking of etiquette as much as she could.

"How did it go?" said the whiny man.

Mme Gauthier laughed. "Will you go in and teach kissing and curtsey, Monsieur Varenne?"

Monsieur Varenne was a beautician of highest reverence in Paris. He burst into the room right away with bad impression and a constant stream of yelling. "Ah Monsieur, you judge me in my fashion because I have better taste than you, which you think I steal from Monsieur Servat. I know my coat, he knows his coat, and he won't tell me the way things are to him. I worked for him for two years and I can't remember most of it in this hour." Monsieur Varenne was getting upset with me as I demanded his credentials. "Why do you always speak of something else when I answer you? Well Monsieur, this is why my question might be the wrong one. The music of Narcisse Girard was used to pass the time because I can no longer think out loud. Monsieur, I am not like de Bergerac, they do not travel to see me and my snout, they are coming from all over the world but you talk all alone. You don't know how to speak to them all, you say it by screaming through your nose, but you shouldn't, Monsieur. Monsieur, I notice that you like very much to answer with your hands, twiddle your thumbs, and as well as it may be, I don't like you, I am just here to do my duty. I'm charity to you. Be patient two minutes and I will give you a cigarette, and I will sing you a verse of Miss Julie and you will listen to me."

Monsieur Varenne tugged on my tie and buttoned up my shirt. "I was asked to do this. But they told me there are things I can and cannot say to you. Develop a more striking memory within him, get him to pay attention to values out of the door they said. Tell him to think like that painting he does with voluptuous incontinence of a brush that is more than intoxicated with the caresses of the flesh. It's all for you they tell me so repeat after me—yes, monsieur—no, monsieur—don't look at me, Monsieur, look between my eyes— look at me, do not look around like a lowlife not looking in the eyes or face of someone when I look at the whole. Are you a peasant too low to explain yourself? Monsieur, I adore my beauty shop, it's my greatest of loves with all its fabrics and equipment. The worst crime I can commit takes place when francs come in and blackheads go out, though it's a just system, Monsieur, some lie and come back to battle at night. I get dressed but my disposition makes me fight those people. I hate them. I don't like them anymore and they are never allowed back again. I did nothing wrong to them and I wasn't made to be taken advantage of at such an advanced age, it's unfair."

He put his hands onto my shoulders and squeezed tightly. "Monsieur, Mlle Phèdre is nice and she likes to laugh. She has superb taste, accepts everyone, and she makes us accept those people. Phèdre would sit down and eat with all of the ordinary people. I understand very well, Monsieur, because I am not stupid, but I speak, I understand, I know that they know you cannot speak to them and that's because they don't interest you, Monsieur. But it's more than that, you are not a great talker aside from what you're skilled in. For me and for you, this will be the most beautiful day of our lives. I lived within my beauty shop for the past four months now because it is the wedding day for the most beautiful woman in France. To dress you and her on what should be the most beautiful day of your life will make me content but I am alone here. Monsieur, where are you? Where did you go? I went on thinking I would be polite to you, that I would share my things with you that I loved and that I love still so much. Why must I give my things to others only to be undervalued? They die with you, they always die with your kind, and you shoot their nerves when you don't care. How much can the beauty Phèdre have really touched you with her royally-sincere and justly inspiring wing?"

Monsieur was too busy making eternal and arbitrary pronouncements with all its apparent syllogisms whose conclusions had always come out of nowhere. His large belly was guided by a worn-down waistcoat. He laughed in such a way that had me rather concerned. He guffawed and his pate reddened, swelling the arteries in his neck and making him quiver as much as his jowls.

"Have you been swept from the pits of Hell by someone who had no reason to care who you were? Do you know what it feels to be fully loved, not by necessity but by sheer will and work?"

He left the room defeated. He turned back. "It takes more firmness of spirit to smile during a wedding than on the field of battle."

All that remained was a review of the final banquet and bouquet. I knew that chaos waited for me in the next few days.

Solly offered up a drink he called gurgur, it tasted like butter. He said he learned the recipe up in Tibet many years ago, sitting around fires, where gardens were on the roofs and the goats slept upstairs in the house. Solly implemented the gardening idea in his own way. He had both a garden on the flat ground and on the roof of his shack. If there wasn't a wired wooden fence, it would be difficult to tell where it all began. There were carpets of blue gentian buds, mauve daisies, bunches of ragwort, cascading pink coral flowers and each flower grew rich in profusion. I noticed red currants, surely sweet to the taste and apricots in the garden.

"Gurgur," I choked on my words. "Did I say it right?"

Solly laughed heartily. "All I'm hearin' is burga. Makin' me hungry for some home cookin'."

"You said you're from Mobile?" I asked, though I knew the answer already.

Solly was almost done tearing up the dry root. He was looking out into the valleys. The view was beyond beautiful. The hills were wet and green where the sunshine fell in heaven-kissed beams and misty clouds walked over the valleys, ignoring them. Solly left the question alone. "The Lord God planted a garden up on the roof of the world."

"That he did," I responded. "It's beautiful."

"Belladonnas have become a nuisance here though." Solly let out a sigh. "They poppin' up errwhere. Neva thought they be too much growin' all 'round me. It's not even full, it's patchy like the green foxglove."

"It can't be that bad, having all this brush," I said, taking a seat next to him with a muffled grunt. "It's rather pleasant to the eyes."

"It's bad for walks, the grasshoppas hide in there an' swarm out w'en you go by. It's like I'm trapped up here sometimes."

"Tell me about Mobile," I asked again, tapping my foot rhythmically on a sward of grass.

"What can I say?" Solly wrapped his arms around his knees which were pressed against his chest. "Mobile is a differn' place. Most the streets, two persons cannot walk abress on the sidewalk for they only a foot an' a half wide. In almost all places, when you pass someone, they gotta step down into the street, and you know that was me. That was me always havin' to make way. Whether it be for a large white folk or lil' ol' ladies on they way to church. To make thins worse, you often come to a dog, sleepin' on the narrow sidewalk, and you either gotta step ova him, but sometimes they bitecha. Too many times have I been forced to walk in the street."

"Is that why you came here?" I said half-jokingly.

"Yeah, back in January of '17," he stated.

"You were escaping the war?"

"So much of it," Solly said, biting his lip and looking to the sky. "War is unjust but lil' folk do in their nerves cuz we contrary to our nature. We can say that's why and that's why and this's why. Nigra gentlemen are the worse though, contradicting every black bone with fightin' and bein' forced to fight."

"Solly," I interrupted. "I left France in 1911, I was one of the lucky ones. I made my way across Europe, I didn't see anything until I hit Nanjing just this past month." I picked up a stick and started tapping at the sward of grass in front of me.

"I lived in Nanjing. I just came from that way."

I froze, dropping the stick. It couldn't be true. "Oh my God."

Some pheasants spread across the sky with their hoarse cries looking for a new stoop to conquer.

There was to be an audience of over two hundred guests composed of leaders in the spheres of politics, royalty, men and women of literature, the representatives of universities, revered journalists, women of fashion, high-gambling Bourse men, and high-finance silk barons, along with many others.

Phèdre was talking with one of her wedding consultants: "I told them, I told them again and again, Villefranche would have been a better destination for the wedding, a place where more merry hours could be spent with a larger crowd. Staunch parents like mine are more concerned with the politics of the country than they are with us."

I was standing in the dining room and Phèdre was on the furniture that I dared not sit on: tables of ebony, chairs upholstered in ruby colored monograms on a cream colored background. She was surrounded by a mixture of eighteenth century furniture, oriental bibelots, and impressionist paintings (few had her eclectic courage). Phèdre was beyond stressed at that moment. Most of the wedding was planned by her and her team. On the 17th of January, 1911, she had already sent forty letters with a seal on which were inscribed the words: *Discret et plein d'espoir.* She also had plenty more to go. Planning the rest of the wedding had to be delayed, for her hands were too busy counting tables on her fingers. Phèdre knew how to be a hostess and was well aware that her family could become social outcasts if she did not seat the guests properly. If people were seated below their rank, she would be cast aside. The guests were to be announced one at a time, the most important were announced first, then a respectable pause, then next. The first to be announced usually left last. Phèdre told me this was the way it has been and always will be.

She was all grace, all gentle response, and all woman. She could seem unpleasing at first to the untrained eye, but she would become much more comforting as soon as she spoke and gestured. She had the energy of a field marshal and could have easily been the ruler of the demi-monde if her morals let her stumble that way. She could make the most prestigious man a bumpkin when he looks upon on her hard work.

At twenty-six, Phèdre de Belzunce was France's leading woman of letters and a formidable champion of liberal ideas. She was also from a royal background which made her enormously rich. Her father, Louis de Belzunce had come from the deepest annals of French Counts and he himself had personally been a financial minister to the King at a young age. His father had worked against the revolution and poured out immense sums of money. Her parents being heavily influenced in the Dreyfus affair had been strict anti-Semitic Republicans that Phèdre wanted nothing to do with. She found herself siding with positivists and the secular kind more often than not. Phèdre attended a noted liberal school, École Alsacienne on the Avenue Vavin near the Luxemborg Gardens. She attempted to break free from the stultifying monotony of her parents' world, an afterthought for the men she was used to being surrounded by (the usual ornamented men who constantly barraged and surrounded her father).

Luckily the tide of France was turning and her endeavors could prove to be fruitful. Though she truly believed a good name was better than a golden girdle—her ambition for wealth and desire to prosper—her own methods carried her soon so far as to drive away the most honest of businessmen. There were no others courageous enough to be devoted to her causes.

Her mornings were occupied by rhythmic exercises, massage, beauty, culture, the hairdresser, and the manicurist at midday. She exercised more, then swam. Her afternoons were a swirl of various activities, by night she was worn out, as she laid on the couch and had books read to her. On those afternoons, she either occupied some form of charity bazaar, social calls, or she was at her salon. People assumed she was running a salon but to be more accurate, it was more like she was presiding over an affectionate foyer. She was usually found waiting for her coterie of regulars along with short-lived celebrities of current tastes and the usual sprinkling of well-born women as well as physically hungry politicians. Some have told me that the breakfast of our honeymoon would be the only meal to which no one will be invited. She once told two well-known salon hostesses,

Mme Cohl and Mme de Fauré, that she loved the experience of dining outside her home to prove to herself how much more people enjoy being guests than hosts. By the womenfolk, she was acknowledged with distance and with the most furtive of glances being conversed about with midday husbands in casino baths. She referred to the other women as megalomaniacs as they mounted theater performances that lasted much too long and meals that were four to six hours exhausted. I have seen Phèdre do hundreds of foolish things within the short time I knew her and they were all charming though because they were perfectly natural. Yet this woman, so indifferent about what she said or did in her salon was unlike all others and was remarkable for her propriety in all important matters. She kept an excellent salon, gave delightful suppers, but she went out rarely and scarcely ever to other parties, though she always received a great deal of company.

Phèdre moved from her seat and stretched her arms out on the cold table in front of her head, looking down at her arrangement with elbows locked. She pushed aside a woven basket full of small gourds and moonworts so that she could see me from where I was. She caught my eye and smiled wearily. Her hair was the color of a Havana cigar and her waist was wasp-like in her sideless curcote, but she moved as gracefully as a Siamese cat. She had grey eyes, beautiful grey eyes and a deep olive complexion. She had a magnificent face, a voice that resonated to the heavens and she was always lively in her movement. She was picking at fine chocolates from Marquise de Sévigné. "To know the art of paying quiet attention, to creatively listen, these are the gifts of a successful host." As she spoke, the soft tone of her voice had a languor in it that went directly to the heart. I returned the smile and gave her a kiss.

Artists served her for two purposes, first for the decoration of her château and then for the establishment of the reputation she was quite eager to protect. Her love of fine arts and her ability to decorate for the wedding were included. Phèdre had always been fond of that which pleased her eyes. In her youth, she had mentioned a brief spurt of painter's whim, she had given it up quickly to her own demise, she traded it in for a distinguished ability to sense talents in old museums and haunted antique shops. She spent most of her early years shopping around for friends and family, collecting an abundance of works. No one has said that she did not have exceptional visual taste. To outsiders, it would certainly look like I was only marrying Phèdre for her name and for her fortune, where it may have actually been reversed.

I stood up and stretched out. The rock I was on felt hard and uncomfortable. I walked to the edge of the cliff and Solly sat still. I looked down to witness the fairy touch of Spring. Beautiful bushes of tamarisk waved their prolific featheries in the breeze in a setting of green fields of dense poplars below in the valley.

"It was a tough time. They was sayin' that we d'int have a choice, we would all be fightin' this war, no subs 'loud or nuthin'. On June fif', I was turnin' twenty-two and they said, they said I had to register and that Nigra's like myself were goin', they ain't any way round it they say. I weren't married, no kids either. All my fella nigra's, they wanted to win the respeck of the white folk. They were gonna fight and win respeck. They were gonna die and have respeck. What good is that? What good is respeck then? Some say this would change thins, that we would be considered equal, that we could fight side by side with white men and die equally, they musta all had short memories, they forgotten the cannon fodda we'd always been? A misplaced enthusiasm. Ninth, Tenth, Twenty-fo', Twenty-fif', they braver men than me, but fools too." Solly clamored on as he clasped his hands together. "I loved my country, but not enough to die ova in some otha place fo' my time. And therefo' I couldn't have none of that. I had saved up enough money workin' at a diner. So I paid a Creole man to take me away, far away. He had a cargo boat and was headin' to Seattle, to pick up some gooey-duck and then to Japan and China he was goin'. He would hide me, keep me company and all I had to do was give him all of my money."

Solly began to rub his hands together for warmth. "That's all I could afford. The cargo boat looked like a giant floatin' morgue, this big, steel, cold, imposin' thing. This boat made stops all around the world, it had earned its stripes and stars. I took the bus down from Alabama and got on the boat on a Sunday night. They said the first stop was Panama. They let me on board and they gave me my own room, but juss in case they were inspecked by someone, they had a lil' box they could stuff me in, all the way on the bottom of the boat. I had to hide in it errtime we docked on sho' for a few hours. Times were getting dangerous and security was tight all around. We went through the Panama Canal first, I made my way to deck, even at night I would be out there, it was pitch dark and nothin' could be seen. I got up err mornin' at fo', dressed, and went up to find humid drizzles of rain. But I could see clusters of lights as we came up on Gatun Lake, maybe it was Limon Bay, I dunno, I know they said we passed the Gaillard cut already. The skies were overcast, which made thins tolerable. I was sick of the glare on deck, off the walls. The sea was rough, spanking the boat like punishment. They let me get off the boat in Panama, to enjoy the life, nobody there would be lookin' for me. It was hot as Hell's embers but so pretty. Being on board wasn't bad at all. Coulda been worse. I won first prize anytime we played dominoes. One guy ended up givin' me his mahogany pistol in a bet. I didn't want it. It was a good bunch of men on board, I coulda been lifelong friends with any of them. But I loss alotta them on the way. Some got off in San Fran, others in Seattle. It was down to me and Liu. The atmosphere on the cargo ship changed after errone was gone, but Liu was there and was a great friend to me. The Chinese seem like a good lot, I thought to myself back then. Good God, I was right. He was a peach of a roommate. These Chinese, they treat you differently, they don't care about yo' skin or nuthin'. I lost him in Shanghai though. We were traveling about 300 knots every twenty-fo' hours 'cept for stoppin' places. I could hear Shanghai on the radio transmissions. I thought it was sumthin' else, I thought we close to Japan or sumthin'. But we skipped pass that and went straight for China, it was Shanghai. Fo' a while I had to sell oil lamps when we arrived. I had to pick up the language quick. I was the only dark man I'd eva seen here. It was imposin' at first. But soon 'nuff they was busy with Russians bein' all over the place. It was mighty hard. I slept on a mud kong, with a fire underneaf for warmth, those nights were so cold, there weren't ever enough peanut shells to burn 'neath me. I bathed in this large earthenware pot like lobsta, the pot was dis high and dis wide. I had to pull myself in, they called it a Soochow tub cuz it was from there. A lil' servant would bring me buckets of hot water, endless numba until that pot was full, ready fo' me to boil. Though Shanghai was dirty, and poor, it had energy and peace."

"How long did you stay in Shanghai?" I asked. "I haven't made my way over there yet."

"Juss til I was comfortable in my skin and tattered cloth," Solly said. "Errthin' was different. The teef on the carpenter's saw was sloped in a different direction. I could go on. It all took sum gettin' used to. Shanghai was hot though. Takin' the rickshaws was fun. But I wanted more adventure, how long could I make it here? I wanted to test myself in the Himalayans."

"I'd rather expect you're talking rot."

"No lies, I have in me the germs of a fulfilling life," he replied. "Can't a man be put out into the deep and succeed?" Solly laughed, showing his teeth. He stroked his head with his sweaty hand, running fingers through his course hair. "I was made for heat but sometimes flourish in frost. I believe I got up as high as eleven thousand, maybe a lil' more. My body is flesh, not brass, my senses danced, and boy they did grumble often. That was my limit. In my time in Tibet, they toll me sumthin', that these mountains are the ring finger of God. Why? Cuz the ring finger is the cleanest finger, it doesn't see much or do much. They taught me all I know about makin' the bess of thins up here. With the farmin' and the gardenin' and not wastin' a thin."

"You stayed in China?" I asked, deeply fascinated. "Did you make it to Nepal?"

"Made it to India and made my way back right after. So after I left the mountains, I made my way North and East. I stayed up in Chungking for some time, had enough of the cold. Enjoyed the rivers there. I visited the French Embassy, nestled between the rivers. That's just before I met the love of my life."

Wildly geometrical flower beds, edged by the fritillaries, hung like lanterns in the sky. Marble tubs in the garden filled with hortensias were watched by statues washed with verdigris. I walked between the clumps of rhododendrons interspersed with Gothic coffers. There were rows of oil lanterns standing high as the light rolled onto the garden, chopping up shadows onto the lawn. The light set upon the rambler roses and marble tubs, a portion with Japanese dwarfed trees, miniature oaks, century old pines, and delicate small maples, none bigger than a head of lettuce. Some guests were early and stroking the trees as if they were delicate cats on the foot of a bed. The men made their way to the parterre in full suits, down a winding path past a birdcage that once housed Charles Augustin de Columb's pet canary.

The Belzunce estate was surrounded by villas bought to mark the stages of triumphal ancestral progress throughout history. Theaters outside with big open flowery spaces dabbled the paths. There was a grape harvest in September which produced about 2,200 bottles of red wine every year. The Jockey Club was in full force searching for stables on the property.

"Did you hear?" a boorish, plain-looking gentlemen asked. "Couston Lake in the eastern part of South Africa is surrounded by a very rich subsoil and that it has luxurious future in the production of tin and other minerals."

"I would invest if it weren't for my loan shark. He's quite the sleek and smooth Shylock." The gentleman struck a piece of cantaloupe with an ivory toothpick.

I walked in the back door to the chaos ensuing within, realizing how big houses are more demanding than humans, especially with a wedding occurring in less than an hour. Inside there were hundreds of candles in ancestral candelabras as they prepared for the reception. Gold place plates, baroque centerpieces, and successive services lined the hallways. The tables were covered in peach cloth glimmering through God gauze. On the mantelshelf of the fireplace near the austere table there were the names of guests fashioned in a particular order, being prepared by a lion of the season. Phèdre had given the responsibility to her closest friends and business partners. She dared not entrust her sisters with this task.

Out on the road, waiting to pick me up and send me to the church was an aristocratic Calvary troupe, a brush of lautrecs and cochers perched on the jump seats of phaétons ready to go, each accompanied by two gray Arabs with flowing manes and long tails plaited with ribands.

Solly stood up and went inside his shack. The orange sky flecked with soft white clouds. Tucked within the fleecy cloudlets, where sky and hill met on the border of the poppy fields, there were watercourses accompanied by razor sharp slits of vetches and purple milkworts. The green slopes were ordinarily verdant and off in the distance. There was a scattering of goats and sheep brought here to pasture on the swards of grass interwoven between patchy yellow primulas. Between the green turfed flats and rugged cruel pinnacles of rock pointing upward to the sky like columns of earth thrown up, there was a yellow glory of poplars. Solly came out with a bag full of barley and a flint. He also offered me a snuff-box. I declined. He began to light the fire as night was coming on us. He sat down and leaned into the rock circle. "This place like a bad oven in summa," he said. "At least it's coolin' now." He handed me an apricot.

"So you have been in love, Solly?" I asked.

Solly closed his eyes, while he began to strike the flint. "Cupid will havt pawn his arrows with me."

"If this isn't a subject for you, then speak no more; if love is not for you, it is not for me either."

"I've been taxed to have lov'd but that was far yesterdaisies," he said. Solly was looking up at the crimson riot of sky above him, his throat protruding outward toward the clouds. "You asked, Jules."

"I did, Solly."

"These dry lids might wanna borrow." There was a somber look on Solly's face as he spoke, I made sure not to move.

"He who has tears, let him." I could barely feel the words leave my lips.

Solly began to tear up. "Afta Chungking, I made my way East, to Nanjing. I got there in 1930, it was a hot summa day when I finally arrived in this large city. I enjoyed it more than I did Shanghai. I'm pretty sure I was the only nigra they eva seen, but that fine wit them. Well, most of them. Juss like any place some them don't like Americans like me, no matter skin colla. But most juss saw me as a spectacle and a person at the same time. I sold newspapers there. I was pickin' up language pretty well, I could hold some conversations you see, but I really ain't eva had a friend so I was all 'bout them niceties at first, *how ya doin', ya welcome sir, nice weatha we havin'* that was it. I had to learn, ain't metta person who spoke English. It wasn't until I met Meixiang that changed. She came to my stand errday. She always wanted a magazine and *Shanghai Xinbao.* The magazine was monthly and the newspaper was weekly and dats all she got. But she came errday and she smiled all the time. She smiled at me, first she looked at me like I was a zoo animal. But errday went by and she said more and more and she teach me stuff. She teach me words I couldn't even say right. She started bringing me tea. She walk ova errtime even though she lived at least six li's away. She worked on the Yangtze River with her sister. Ya see, they helped her father run a restaurant. She sat people, she waited on them, she cooked, and she did it all. She would come to me errday. She was the tallest Chinese woman I'd seen my whole time here. She had been closer to six foot than anybody else. She scared people off, I'm thinking errtime they come around. It's intimidatin' to see a woman, especially that tall in China; Lordy I got only an inch on her. But that's why she liked me. I wasn't scared a her. I liked her. I liked her dark long hair and deep bangs on her fo'head. Her teeth were a lil' crooked but so are mine. Her smile was heaven on earth. And she gave it out to errone. When she told me where she work, I went there again and 'gen. We played lil' cat and mouse fo' a while. We eventually got married on the Yangtze in 1931. We moved in her father's house. He loved me. They had a house big 'nuff fo' mo'. But it was just me, Meixiang, Dad, and Sister 'til Sister Ziu got married. Meixiang lost her mother to typhoid fever when she was juss a kid. Meixiang and me were perfectly useless to each other. When we spoke of the world, we spoke of two different worlds, they barely were the same. But that was okay, with all the fright we learn thins wit one 'nother. Sumtimes I find her by a chorten, on her knees loss in prayer. She said she didn't need to be in prayer to see the bad that was comin' our way. She's always said, that I was her guest and she'd do all she could to save and protect me."

The priest was well fed with a walrus mustache and blubber lips. The words came from his bristles like crumbs of dry bread. He shouted with lungs of leather though his voice had an extraordinary sadness. "Repeat after me. We promise to consecrate our lives to each other—we declare that we regard ourselves as indissolubly bound to each other—that we shall share forever and in every respect a common destiny—that we will never enter into any other bond so long as you shall live—and that you shall strengthen the bonds now uniting us as soon as lies within our power—and the power of our Lord and Savior Jesus Christ. Amen."

The priest's mustache began to droop. "Now I've heard that you two would like to say something to one another, perhaps we can bestow God's blessing on those who rapped on the door of liberty with the myrtle wand of love." He looked at Phèdre. "Mademoiselle de Belzunce, I give you the honors," he said turning to her.

Phèdre retrieved a folded paper from her bosom. She unfolded the paper, fighting back the tears. "My whole life, men have come to me asking for my love but they daren't woo me. They made promises, but those men daren't stay with me. I called out to them, but they daren't visit me. Te voilà mon Bourrienne. Tu aussi seras immortel for the God Cupid has struck me to the bone. The stress and agitation caused by the uncertainty of this wound tossed me into a sort of fever that I was feigning. We call this passion. I find that when I am not near you, everything wounds me. When intimacy peaks, we can find joy in the private jokes and little things that pair us as one, the things which hold captive the heart with thousands of ties." Phèdre turned toward the congregation. "I found haven in his proud timidity which often makes Julian silent in company. But his mind is lively and more serious than one can mature alone. Your speech instead portrays charm and resourcefulness. When we are to be alone, I am beside myself with happiness at the person you become when the mask is off. I understand you because I resemble you because I understand what it is like to make the voyage of life partially alone. I do not wish to die like Rousseau. I want the sun for many more years if I may pursue life by your side. I want my days to end by your feet like these waves who murmur your love. Heaven had created us for one another. We were to meet and fly together like mountain birds. With the memory of the times of exquisite delight you have given me, I have built within my heart a chapel filled with you. And it is there I will love you until time ends."

The priest cleared his throat looking uncomfortable and hot as he shifted his shoulders. "Go ahead, Monsieur," the priest said. "Go with God, show your wife your love."

There in front of me was Phèdre, the rest of my life, and everything else. The passing torch of the wonders of the world were in her nuptial veils. There may have not been anything else to have been had then and there. Phèdre was a young soul, young heart, but the years were all there.

"We are all members of a French Nation devoted to the guises of Eros," I began, feeling quite nervous in front of all these people. I felt the heat of my blood in my chest. "All women I have possessed are no more than a mattress for the woman of my dreams. Love is a game of anticipation and wits which add to its piquancy. I was always told the ideal woman was the exquisite, perfectly dressed Parisienne, an agitated woman conflicted by the teagown beauty crayoned in by Degas, who swirled through the hush of taffetas and the soft rustle of satins and whatnot. You my dear, are the ivy leaf of oceans. Ten thousand treasures I wanted that France couldn't provide to me and all those, vapid, negative things appeared but I never thought love was for me but now I know love is an essence. Love is an essence, yes, but all its instances are accidents, none being necessary to the essence as such. My life, my life has been made up of a few outpourings. All these channels, they have a mouth of coming together. You are the mouth of coming together. There is no other. I feel like the only one you can give play to in all your ideas, morals, and thoughts. Love things lightly as you tread, take in that which you see, and to the winds with guilt and regret. Let them feed into what it is to be lulled by the waves if no other sounds in France. Let early youth sing the charms of love. Let life later prime the storms of oncoming war. Try to guess at the inks that went into an acrylic painting about the soul, you bring to me in private and France in public. I love you, Phèdre."

We kissed before the priest could speak and seal the holy vow. The cheer of the congregation sounded like a tolling bell.

"Meixing is tough," Solly said, warming his hands by the fire. "She is a tough lady derservin' of marriage. Ought never does the wife have to follow the husband 'cuz which is stronger of the two spouses? Who truly is the one who holds the snath and grip in they hands? The one cookin' meals, the one gatherin' pears to make cider, the one fermentin' for tipples, they be qualified for brandyin'? Meixiang's pipe gives off more gas than mine. Would a man swim longer than his wife? Can't even be jealous of that, it'll splinter up a marriage," Solly started placing logs into the fire pit as he spoke. "The presence of Japan was gettin' ever stronger. Meixiang was 'fraid fo' me. We were seein' thins errwhere. If it wasn't the Reds, it was the Japs. They had to hide me in the basement. We decided I had to leave Nanjing but I just wanted to stay with my wife. They had been droppin' leaflets all over, they said war was imminent, we had all talked about war 'nuff, it's about time we all shut up. It's toxic and goin' back over it stirs the poison brew. All our tongues shoulda be black by the arsenic, mixed with dirt and our own sweat. No more hubbub and grand swooping gestures there, even the whispers seem devious and scheming like nasty lil' ditch soldiers. On my way outta Nanjing, err once in a while the pohlease they would capture ahole group and throw them in the back of a pickup, all them were tied up, you see. The officers, they would stage a parade of sorts, with bugles blarin', it got errone attention. When the truck comin' up to a populated corner of the road, one of the people, they dumped out, they stan' 'em up, that's usually hard though cuz on account all the dope they be given, it's a lil' mercy beefo they get shot in the head. I saw it once, a woman sprawled out bleedin' like a fountain in the dirt. I saw them pull on the next corner and do the same thin. We lived juss outside of Nanjing. We had to get away. Meixiang would make her way back to see to the restaurant. She kept me there hidin'. She brought me a tasteful soup. It tasted like veal but she said it was Shantung dog, it was the only food around anymo'. She told me it was that or starvin'. She said the peasants believed that anyone who ate Shantung dog became possessed by the spirits which that dog had harbored itself, fo' seven years you had that spirit in you. I said we all did, we all harbored spirits of loved ones and others. After a while stayin' the stench of urine and dirt stuck to my bones. With Meixiang gone for weeks, I had not a crumb of comfort, not a speck. I know she went for supplies and to help her father out, to see how Sis was doin' but she was takin' too long. She promised to protect me though. What about me? I thought. I should protected her."

The tears began to flow from Solly's eyes. He tried to fake it out by turning away as he spoke. Solly stood up and I followed. We were there for a while, staring off into the falling sun, and there around it were two perfect and complete halos. He went to the shack, he came back with more wood, broke a bundle of twigs over the fire ready to speak of the affinity of madness even more as his tears began to dry up. I remained silent.

"I had to make my way back to find her. But I wasn't stupid. Imma nigra, I stan out. I camped above the city—on the outskirts—a familiar place. There were days back beefo war, where we could sit and watch the lanterns on the boats, makin' twistin' colors on the waves from up high. The voices of what looked like ants, going home from a day's hard work in the fields, loudly spoken which was owin' to some strange acoustic relationship between the crags and the valleys on the opposite side of the fields. But those days were gone. The Yangtze was owned up by General Chiang and his drug troops movin' crack. Have you seen but a phosphorescent lily grow before rude paws have touched it? All was loss, but I still had to try. I moved by night and you could see there were globes of fire that caused so much terror in me. By tricks of fire licks, everyone seemed bodiless and hoverin'. I had to make my way down. I had to find Meixiang. First I had to cross the Yangtze or make my way around. I wasn't good swimmin' but many boats been abandoned on that side of the river. I made my way quietly. You see people had still been attemptin' to flee. I saw there before me a shadowy figure with a put-out lantern crossin' the river as their raft of twigs bumped hard on the shore, attempting' to detach itself from the fir branches. They sobbed quietly. I saw missin' fingas on they hands. I don't know how they been paddlin'. They musta been gettin' stuck on all the broken trees floatin' around. I hit the sho on the other side. There on the sand, not far from the grass, a human skull wit-out a jaw or half their eye socket. The skull was rotten with skin still clung despite the chugging winds, there was a broken blade goin' through the remainin' socket. The pieces of flesh were all 'round. I crawled up an embankment and crouched real low to see the houses on fire. Of the faces that came out of the conflagration, as if painted black, barely mobile from the distance of yellow reds, the most noticeable was a young man's face beaten and broke. He had looked defeated, uncaring, and unapologetic. Out came a few soldiers, from the flames which seemed to lick them. They wore semi-military outfits, but they were lookin' more like Ronins in the flames. A soldier took that young man by his long greasy hair, pulled on it, kicked him to his knees. The background was vacuumed by the glare as a hand descended from the wavy darkness, thrust on his head and lopped back and fo'ward 'til there were only a body. Shouts of laughter came from the reactionary few, some before others. They garnished his head on barbed wire so it stuck as they hung it from a poplar tree. It thumped the bark on accounta wind. But that wasn't nothin' to nobody. I ain't never known what it's like takin' 'vantage of someone. I'd always been on the wrong side of that. I saw blood flowin' in the guttas. My shoes, my socks, my trousas, errthin was caked in blood, the heat made it dry up quick. I saw charred skeletons in the houses still grippin' they children. You know, it wasn't seein' the dead babies, it wasn't seein' all the death or destruction neitha, it was how they was takin' 'vantage of the women. I could see by the fire's light what they were doin', burlap sacks over they heads, not knowin' if it was the same guy or different one now. I never in my long life wanted to die 'cept then and there. I wanted to get out from under cover and run at 'em all. I wanted to lurch their way and rip off every head they had. But that was certain death. I wasn't that stupid, but I saw Meixiang in errface. Every Chinese face was Meixiang. My eyes were so clouded wet, I couldn't make out faces anymore. I called her name through all my tears with a barely heard whisper as I made my way to the mounds of bodies. I hoped someone was alive and knew her. I woulda danced a jig of joy right there, right on spot, if I coulda seen her face one mo' time, even if lifeless. If I could have held her one more time in my arms, Jules, I woulda been okay with bein' shot, decapitated, or anythin'. This moment, it's so hard to remember, to call back, not cuz it's difficult—that makes it easier to recall in sleepless nights—it's an absolute hovel, where no one understands the chaos and it at times has nothing to want to do with us. We want this death and destruction to be final, and give us answers. But it ain't doin' that. All the niggling self-doubts that we brush aside, all the uncertainty that brings on sadder grones, being put down in order to force ourselves into perfect moments of understanding, these moments make me wanna believe she's still out there somewhere. Whichever way one turns, the lump is ever there, and blood will curdle on moment's notice. A known evil compared to nothingness is beautiful and grand. I juss wanna know. I just wanna know those last moments. Was she a victim of cannibal banquets? Did she escape?" The tears were like a leaky faucet coming off Solly's nose, he bent down and let them leak into the fire pit.

I was drawn in by his words, his horrific tale, unable to speak myself.

"That day we married," he continued. "At the stroke of midnight, she told me she could hear the crimes of Nanjing and her dreams told her of the thins that happened in the dark of night. One day we walked in the fields along the Yangtze, admiring the beauty of it, the silence of Nanjing and she turned to me and said, *You must tell all of this. There are things you need to know. And love, you must tell all of this.*" Solly sobbed into the fire. He no longer held back.

They were near the end. Guests of the wedding ceremony had made their way back to the château de Belzunce. They were being announced one by one: *Duke of Rothesay which was the newly appointed Edward who was also the Prince of Wales and Earl of Chester. Duke of Cornwall. Earl of Carrick and Duke of Brandon.* I will never forget when they called in the minister of arts and director of the Louvre, Théophile Homolle. He was distraught and the topic of much conversation that night. Detectives were still looking for the *Mona Lisa*.

"My life has been a shambles, and I have been cast out for my earlier comments. I shall be forced to give up Notre Dame now since I have been maneuvered out of my place there," the minister said. "I won't make it to the next Vernissage if we don't find the perpetrator of my downfall." Beads of sweat were dripping off his nostrils. Theo, since entering the room had been giving deep looks the way of Guillaume Apollinaire all night long, even at Trinity he scouted him out. "I will not go out with the hoop skirt and a bustle. I am loath to think of losing it all."

In the background, guests were still being

announced:

"Jacques Doucet—Coco Chanel—Valentine Hugo—Blaise Cendrars—Jean Cocteau—André Gide—Marie Bashkirtseff—Carolina 'La Belle' Otero—Cléo de Mérode — "

The central cloister of the château was spacious and attractive. It had an enclosed formal parterre shaded by tall acacias. Far off, the orchestra and dance floor were still being set up. Mysterious séance tables had been set in odd places. Every room in relation to the open space was themed and stuffed with amusing knickknacks. Black and Moroccan maids and butlers rushed from the kitchen to set plates, early Sèvres designs of burgundy Marly. Some were carrying silver platters full of wonderful foods and Venetian finger-bowls with their edges festooned with baroque pearls serving up madeleines, marrons glacés, and petite rissoles à la viande.

Prince Mohammed Ali Tewfik was in the corner of the room leaning against the wall somberly talking with the Duke of Hamilton; they matched one another in their tobacco colored-clothing. I had heard about Mohammed being a childish sovereign. He would be found in Pacy-sur-Eure grouse shooting for sport every month but he would say, *The family doesn't like it if I come to France too often.* He had a devilish smile of superiority when he talked even to the Duke. I had learned the Prince wrote Phèdre a letter full of expressions of esteem. He gave her permission to take a withdrawal from his account, but in such a way as to make her understand that this permission was a very much softened royal order. He would eventually sustain his disgrace like an honest man when his country could not afford his extravagance. The Egyptian Prince was making exaggerated movements toward the Duke as he spoke:

"Nothing would be discussed in the home of such droll royalty except the dresses and the hair, a common topic of conversation amongst women when they have nothing else to say to each other, which is often. Women do everything to please one another despite their complete and utterly detested feelings." The Prince's moustache was of the variety that I have come to associate with Third Republic military officials, he actually more closely resembled the provincial stationmaster presiding over this waiting room as if it was his last. The Duke laughed and took a sip of wine. "I expect the food to taste like frizzled corks."

Most of the guests had been already seated for a while because their bones could not take standing and socializing very long. Abstemious women sat down, placing their white gloves in the champagne flutes, and asking for water. The menu for the night was as large of one as could be imagined with potage aux perles, velouté aux nids d'hirondelles, cassolettes morilles (I am unsure which kinds), sauce truite perche over filet de saumons aux truffes, poularde de bresse rosière, jambon de bayonne Provençale, and for desserts there were more choices such as spoom au porto dore, canetons Duclair rôtis Normandie, asperges in sauce mousseline. The chefs presented a special menu for a few guests which included pheasants in white sauce, salamagundi, and cassoulet toulousain. Prince de Sagan had made a special request for bouillabaisse and was served such.

Lady Michaud had arrived too late to take her seat, too busy making passes at every piece of royalty she could find like a chess board while they attempted to pet her aggressive dog. She displayed herself like a statue for everyone to admire, as if carved from delicate porcelain and ivory and set on a dresser to never be touched again. She looked an elegant 1.72 metres and 58 kilos in wet clothes. She had bedecked herself with more gewgaws than I could count while strutting magnificently in a décolletage à la baigmore formal gown which raised more than a few tufted eyebrows. If she wasn't so rich herself, she would be a sycophant but that didn't mean she wasn't on the search for more power. She was after all, a discreet demi-mondaine with a bourgeois concern for respectability. One of the maids had noticed she had not been served any food and offered her the finest foie gras.

"Thanks but I do not partake in swollen animal diseases," she whined. She crushed up some crackers with her fist; they spread across the white linen with a scoop going into the mouth of her toy poodle and another swoop going into her own.

Imperial Mme Michaud, in the name of her Mother Charlemagne and Father Capital Nusmismatic, was fascinated by the eight jewels of the eight wonders of the ancient world, her mother, a great European lady and her gigantic green balcony on the Seine, the English, Normandy, Pays de Caux and on graville abbey, couvent palace and whatnot were the talk of all. Mme Grandmother sipped on her time as the rest outgrew, its walls like cholera and typhoid, like ice-floe in Barents sea. Mme never saw work, only capitol bursts here or there and folds of reflex blue, safe red 032, or the winds of the Atlantic in her salty blockhouses. She was already in conversation.

Lady Michaud had married a Prussain war hero and left him and the child in Marseilles. She stayed with a friend whose morals were lacking and she was soon swept within the cities lights but her beauty was able to save her on multiple occasions. She was united by luck with twenty years of mutual affections. She then met a Spanish Marquis who bore the name of Don Gabino de Martorell; she was to be his mistress and nothing more and he spoilt her tremendously. That wasn't enough for Mme Michaud as she found herself in a love affair with an Italian Court. The rumors swirled about. "He writes to me all the time, they are hollow letters though, dying in longing to find some substance," Lady Michaud said.

Two women were sitting at a table by themselves, young courtesans whispering to one another about the Marshal's wife, Elisabeth de Cannaught. Her husband was Arthur, head field Marshal of the British command. I could barely make out their words.

"I hear she eats the juiciest part of the fish, throws the guts at you, she takes the cheese, she empties the milk without asking if you need some for your day, she takes the moistest part of the cake, she refuses any fillers and takes nearly every lump of sugar." The woman speaking was wearing flapping flounces of white organdy, silver tassels, and a bow of velvet.

It was clear to me that these women did not care for Elisabeth de Cannaught.

"She's open enough to be seduced by our gamekeeper is what I hear. I went over and said such things to her. She bit back and I was not only wounded by her tone but by her words as she called me a grisette," the lady scoffed. "You marry a titled army officer and then call yourself a countess or maréchale or some other title. She had the audacity asking me later on to borrow a sapphire pendant."

We all knew of these type of women, sitting at cafés disparaging their competition with their Parisian flightiness, drama to the marrow of their bones. These were titled ladies, minimally poetry-conscious women with debased literary aspirations, effete but still young. They would swarm into overcrowded, bourgeois salons where men would stand and spin gold aesthetic talks of philosophical ideas and heaps of rich discussions. The women were utterly lost, wishing to return to their native milieu. They wanted to receive engraved invitations topped with three tower crests, they wanted to be invited to hear the poets read selections from their works. These women would always sigh— *How Wonderful!*—over darkly turgid passages they did not even begin to understand and they nodded in assurance over the names of classical personages culled from authors' own private mythologies.

"Did you know she was once so skinny she

would swallow a pea and look pregnant, but now she looks too big and a bit squeezed together in that dress."

The two women continued to laugh at the Marshal's wife.

"Dresses thicken her and even more so spoil her shape."

"Well, that's because everything about her is a little overdone."

"Is this a Hardouin-Mansart?" the one woman asked.

The older woman looked around the room. "These old houses are brick and wood, full of damp and dust."

"But dust is the furniture's face powder, is it not?"

They paused before bursting into a controlled laughter.

On the chairs directly in front of us was the problem of Phèdre's Uncle Gustave and his extreme radical politics. He was currently in an intense discussion with Xavier de Tristan's wife. Phèdre's parents were staunch Republicans, but not as extreme as Gustave, though they all shared the anti-Semitic views that Phèdre's uncle acted upon. Gustave was trapped in the past. He might as well have shown up as a white-wigged, brown-trousered lackey. But Gustave was suffering from a nasty case of gout and had worn his slippers to the wedding. I watched him shuffle around the room throughout the night. His long gray hair was in tone with his stream-like beard. When talking proudly, he would make his eyebrows circumflex in a disgusting fashion. He was truly a man of such slumping posture and unmarital bearings. Besides being strongly anti-Semitic, Gustave was also a staunch opponent of electricity since it was introduced. He researched diligently what he called "an utter abhorrence". He went around telling people that electric light coming from those illuminating globes was bad for a young girl's skin and eyes. He also believed that electricity was the greatest hazard since the poisonous Northern Lights to hit the modern world. He continued to heat his own house with gas as he melted the crinoline and books near the dinner table and by the end of the night, his wife's makeup ran in rivulets.

Gustave sat with his arms crossed, pulling in closer to Madame and he was busy telling her about the time he wrote a letter to the prefect a few years ago declaring his armed intent if those iron boxed automobiles were to get anywhere near his children and wife. He said in this note he would personally hunt down the vehicle and shoot everyone inside. "Never forget that the prefect was of Jewish origin, though he has done everything in his power to make others forget it," Gustave said.

Valérie de Tristan, being born unscrupulous and with very little appreciation of the sweetness of love as happy as that into which she had entered with a virtuous and gallant man was happy to reply to Gustave with more hatred herself. Her face was haggard and her hands looked like ancient claws. There are pleasant old ladies that tell many droll, uninteresting lies about themselves and Valérie was one of those women, that was of course if you had the fuel to flame her passion. With Gustave around, she was suddenly vocal like a golden hive. She had not been given many opportunities for such display. Valérie ran off with Léon de Tristan, a wealthy investor to the sad, prim countryside of Cornheilhan after he had been involved in a financial scandal where she settled in like a soldier who was mortally wounded but had gone on living anyway.

"The French Jews, they have been attempting to lose their characteristics, they understand that they are hunted wanderers but they know how to blend and create an illusion of practicality within our society which certainly has given them the sense of value and pride knowing how to always extract profit from the services they render," Valérie said. "Guess you can say our anti-Dreyfusard tendencies brought our families together while we watched thousands rifted apart."

They clinked their glasses together in a celebratory fashion.

"January 5th of '95 was one of the best days of my advanced life. The entire city was stilled by the cold weather, but spirits were high. We all wore overcoats and huddled together outside the Morland Courtyard. There was something magical when they dragged him out and stripped him of his medals and clothes. Even the children running through the legs of adults enjoyed every moment," Gustave smiled as he continued. "And you know what? We can make it all look like carbon monoxide poisoning like Zola and Syveton."

They laughed out loud like barbarians in harmony.

"Drumont opened my eyes, Gustave," she said. "It's hard to walk past *un sale youpin* and not yell, P-s-s-t! The hooked-nose lechers are like leeches to errand girls. Jesus was a Jew, yeah, to only show humility and imperfections as a human form."

Gustave had a grin on his face which suddenly turned more serious. "Those things on Earth that differ the most should also be the most isolated from each other," Gustave had been drinking and the way his words meshed made it more apparent. He appeared to be sucking on his upper lips between every other sentence. "The Blacks and Whites is what I speak of. The main task of the government was to guard Maubeuge, which represented the gate to Sambre. This entry way seems to have been most vehemently disputed in the course of the past twenty years. However, defending Maubeuge cannot apply to Africa Blacks. It all works for the old world inasmuch it is populated by Whites and they do not come in contact personally with Blacks and the places where they live. The fight to defend the canalized Sabis demonstrates and best confirms the Nigger world discovered by us in our area. The danger of their appearance here in our country was so great that the inhabitants were condemned to constantly eat black rind hoop cheese to express an already existing togetherness with the Blacks. The existence of the coypu demonstrates the effort with which evolution avoids something like it. In this situation, the word *waste* would be linked first of all to the plant in order to make the stem. The Nigger itself is close to the wasteful coypu but the devices of nature and will within the name of the Black is very strong which will impose itself and which tritely means the same thing seeing this up close and comparatively will be impossible because nothing is similar to the Negro. The question could arise, namely, what is a nigger? If we can comprehend, then an obedient nigger is certainly something that is better, better known and could very well be Black and that means therefore the obedient Black exist. But that's wrong. This obedient nigger is wasteful, it is a coypu, and it does not cross the bodies of water on its own. We cannot always see him but it's there, doing damage. They are in our area and as long as they are members of a world of their own. Please take note that the coypu usually does not live past the first year of their lives, they are born underneath our mortality and will live underneath it without having seen or lived here. In this way of life, we are able to recognize a Negro world which exists with us at the same time, in the same area, but different than our own. Until now, it was never possible for one race to invade the world of another and now this is possible. If you have doubts in my statements, I refer you to looking at the lips of the Negro, they protrude outward, and we call them haut. The mouth of the Negro is raised. Those farthest away from home draw nearer to each other under one color. This generally is White."

I could take no more of Gustave's evil words, they were exhausting and each and every pleasantry was nauseating. I escaped outdoors while men were simultaneously quitting their tables to go have a smoke. The women were forced to stay indoors. *Shall we move from this beastly crowd?* I heard a gentleman murmur. A rich baron got up and smirked at Raymond Poincaré as they whisked onward. I found a nice place to lean on the balcony out of sight in the comfortable, cool night.

The young blades were the first to reach the balcony, reserving the seats for the older gentleman in that sarcophagus of linoleum stuffed with mummies, excusing their wrinkles as aged scars. Out there was a soirée of every political spectrum. There were liberal republicans, municipal republicans, opportunist republicans, radical republicans, autonomous radicals, hidden socialist radicals, revolutionary radicals, outspoken anti-Semitic radicals, blanquists socialists, possibilist socialists, and anti-Semitic socialists. There was the feeling of a mutual hatred for Prussia as well as many other things including marriage and the concept of this grand ceremony they had been forced to attend.

Ambroise Thomas was the conservatory coordinator, he was also a home-wrecking, jew-hating, negrophobic, homosexual, failed actor-speech-giving-ice-skater-pets de loup and was the first to speak.

"The prospect and institution of marriage is so goddamned admirable," he lit up a cigar as he spoke. "It's the most enduring challenge in our lives east of survival. It's supplanting a goal which no longer exists and it endures on different interest for you see, man and woman once married stand on opposing terms. The woman finds purpose to her life, her ambition is set toward keeping a man in her sights and never letting go. In that, she feels altruistic and as if she has made sacrifice. In marriage, the man loses his purpose in life that of finding women. His chase, his purpose, is now his bond, his entrapment. It's funny how we never recognize this unequal relationship until it's too late until we cannot get along anymore. Marriage is a good furnace in which to burn a surplus of life not already absorbed up by philosophy and work. How many women the morning after the honeymoon are widows of the husbands they've imagined so well? But I have found the formula for love that lasts for life. Affairs, adultery, ménage is what we call it when one partner loves and the other does not. If neither loves each other *that* is true marital bliss."

A majority of the men found themselves in agreement with Thomas. There wasn't much to be said more on the subject but another man in a putty-colored tussore jacket and beige gaiters with the whiskers of a lion who was smoking a pipe had to chime in. He had looked familiar to me. It might have been the Duke of Gascony, someone who had known the Belzunce family for years.

"You know I've talked with Phèdre since she was a youngster," the Duke's words sounded like a nasal trumpet blast. "She was obsessed with the feminist writings of Edith Wharton and there she decided that listening to her father's marriage advice was utterly tyrannical and selfish. The narrow-mindedness of a Republican mind whose strict views on human emancipation failed to extend past members of any Royal Family name that was pronounceable. At first I believed her quibblings would have simply been part of a rebellious phase of her youth—that of a precociously intelligent lady—but Phèdre had proven to me quickly that this was no phase and her intentions had not been staked in royalty but in the people of France all at once. She would marry them all if she could. All the poor and all the needy." The Duke's language was imperial, not courtly, but brusque and commanding. "And before you go challenging my wits and being offended, similar to an Orléanists nobleman reacting with abhorrence to anything Napoleonic, think about this, the Republic is gone, but this will require a political necromancer to figure out what exists in its place. Do not judge her on her views but her spousal choice is more than worthy of your opinion." He began to wriggle his shoulders and he leant back like a suddenly unmanned rickshaw.

A few men made snarky comments before he continued.

"Phèdre had been bored by the insipid sameness of social life of the typical Republican, the false stilted formalities designed to choke off any real emotion that wasn't hate. She was a stranger to these people and that made her feel incredibly lonely. Phèdre had to escape this as she was sinking further and further into the yawning hole of mental illness. This may have helped her develop a gift, that of poking fun at people without wounding them, it mostly brought smiles to their lips. Nothing is more dangerous than to fill the role of a charming and incredibly beautiful woman. As for Jules, I think his marital future will turn him into the male version of an odalisque. Ligur' aoide, my friends. If I only knew more about him and his spirits."

Pierre Villars had spoken up. He was usually serving penance by his own anxiety. He took cocaine often to untie his tongue. He was a rich bachelor, stingy and economical in his spending habits and he chose to affect the rich with his spending. He would not buy bread off the streets but by that, he hardly bought much. In Paris, he had only an office in which he slept and worked and took his meals. He had turned down a few marriage proposals, two engagements called off, one wedding called off, three phases of getting right with God, double crosses, zigzags, defeated feelings of altruism and junked up self-respect, more of this than your average actor or actress. His mess of a life has not been chronicled yet because it cannot be mentally encompassed. It's too difficult to grasp what was going on there. Pierre was never found without a beret on and he had come to the wedding in white linen and a geranium blazer.

"Jules' paintings speak to us," Pierre said. "He has put everything out there. His realism is a romanticism tempered by pessimism, the pessimism of a man abandoned by his family, left in abortive stances and bitter disappointments. For him, life is extremely stupid but France as a whole is deucedly grand and Phèdre stands as a symbol of such for him. It seems to me, the transient value of his works is also based on the master's imposition on himself to the contemporaries and there he can become fairly content. He can become congenitally happy. I heard his father and mother had abandoned him at birth which clearly attributes to his tendency to melancholia, to suffocating self-reliance and obsessive nomadism. I hear he is also well-versed in German and English. He is currently learning Latin, helping give him a keen ear for music and poetry. So it is not exactly that he is socially déclassé but that he has been squandering his open opportunities and is beginning to lose all his advantages that no one like him will ever be offered again in our lifetimes. Maybe it has something to do with an orphan's fear of being found wanting. He is a fallen man who like Phèdre craves a mystical reinstatement and retribution. He doesn't want to suffer, he hates it but he cannot pry himself away from Campden Hills."

More men were making their way outside to the group, helping to complete this steadfast intellectual constellation. They all would be tirelessly wielding fiery oratorical skill and political acumen most would find deadly, but among equals it felt more like tender arguments excusing themselves as endless dialogues. Young men complained about finances while older men cried over their rheumatisms. The men always tired talking about literature and art so they found other subjects usually leaning toward women, disease, and death. Out came members of the high-priced hierarchy known as Degrafees. The King of Portugal, Emmanuel the Second, the disputed king, sat next to Prince de Sagan Hélie while the rest of the Le Gratin shuffled in. The exclusive elite of the smart, the wealthy, and the well-born including a few who were not so well-born, most of them hailing from

Fauborg, Saint Germain Quarter, Saint François, Xavier or rue des Saint-Pères while some were Kings of ex-madmen, Knights of feathers, and Sorcerers of winds from Carrick with watch chains draped across their middles. These men were to be the last of a dying generation. This was our time, the upper class was now being trained to take over the world that their fathers had broken their backs to create. This world was buttressed by a hard-worn faith in the human capacity for progress and change. Now was the time to be championed by science, by knowing the knowable, by explaining the explainable, this vision was to seep into the world of politics and economics.

I attempted to sneak back inside without being seen. I was caught in the door by Phèdre's mother. She told me the dancing was about to begin and that I was needed. Couples had already been making their way to the dance floor. The orchestra was nearly done tuning and setting up. The grand piano had finally found its way through the entrance with its ebony lacquer carved with blood-red climbing roses. The reflection of the crystal chandeliers and the sheering shine of the girandoles could be seen in the piano, only dulled out by the lush chintz curtains. The Stradivariuses had been un-coffined as a pretty lady bent over the harpsichord tried out alternative fingerings. She was wearing a beautiful jade necklace and matching jade bracelets. Phèdre's own personal harpist had recently been in pain, and Phèdre had ordered a pair of whalebone stays with a little plate of lead placed by her shoulder.

Placed in the center of the room by

Monsieur de Belzunce was a handsome tablet garnished with diamonds in which the center of the piece held the Belzunce coat of arms. Lozana was sitting at a clavichord, gazing at me.

People began to rise from their chairs and harshly the organ replied. I heard an older woman speak from behind me. "I'm sticking to slow dancing in such a burning room. It might be wise to wait until post-midnight to extinguish the party feel."

Some men lurked disconsolately in the background and dismal young daughters awaited rigidly on gilt chairs beside their mothers as the music began to play. The swoosh of crinoline, boas undulated on dresses wrapped around ample busts as the waltz crashed onward. The orchestra played Chopin, Schubert, Gluck, Ketterer and some Spanish songs as the guests danced the farandole, the Consuelo, Napoleonic quadrilles, Versailles minuets, Henri IV pavanes, and the utterly insane brawl of the Vendée. These were the dances, the music, and the fling of her own soul as the dances had the control that would no longer offend Mothers. The techniques were respectable, which might owe itself to the corset, the lacings of that inflexible, stiff bastion of honor.

Ladies-in-waiting made their way out with young bachelors. I always wondered how many happily married couples are estranged by the ceremony itself. The wife left in her seat as the man found excuses for his heart. One couple was found hogging the floor. They seemed like the type you would see embracing on top of a Sèvres tureen. Though she was attracted to his fame and money, she knew nothing about his checkered past but that womanly ignorance certainly lessened the cramping he felt from the restraint his past put on him. One takes notice to the married pair who smile the sweetest to their acquaintances in sights of public, it's those whose countenances bear various scars and scratches commemorating late night orgies at the house to the discretion of musical profanity. With eyes closed, the Andalusian beauty was perspiring in her Saint Cyr dress.

Mlle Colette spun about the room at a distance of only an inch from her partner during the intervals between the quadrilles. She dried the beads of sweat off her throat with white-gloved hands plying with ostrich feathered fans but that wasn't enough as she grabbed a sauce-spotted napkin and began to wipe her face, neck, armpits, and her thighs. Then she'd dance some more. The way she moved was like a sort of aerostatic swell that pushed her along methodically.

There was a man on the corner of the floor in a mauve suit, he was talking to another gentleman with white gloves, top hat, flowered waistcoat, and a high velvet collar with ribboned monocle and a carnation in the button hole.

"It smells of bad junket in here," he proclaimed pressing down his blouse. "The jeune fille has always been one of the most unalluring beings on the continent we live on. These gawky, pasty beasts are nature's 8th wonder of the world. How they slither out from their chrysalises and magically evolve into delicate butterflies of their later married years is truly something none of us will ever understand. This still doesn't deter the groom's mistress from trailing them along during their honeymoon." Before he could finish, he was pulled to the center of the floor by his wife. She dropped a sketchy curtsey to him which allowed the bare flesh of her arms between the edge of her white glove and her bracelet to have a kiss bestowed upon it.

Madame de Cometois danced around like a fallen Boulette d'Avesnes in the Alpen Schinken basket filled with Almoravid Berbers heads, bouchair, bourjeje, and disarmament. Madame caught though like Latouche Tréville (To Girond and Jacob both on white horses) naked (without a green cap) and begging for thé 88lbs clean shave and a brocaded flag with long folds trailing with a head of crowns tied to a carriage. The pale slaughter underneath the musk of the virginal. Out came the clowns in black, dancing to the final three piece by Fortier encored and much applauded. The composer eventually had to come down into the room to greet. The Dance of Seven Veils of Marriage in the orchid bouquet, they said they would bring my head to Herod Father, who was always quenched with incestuous desire—7 airs—on a silver platter. Mme de Belzunce remained on her feet with her beaded spider clappers as a wedding present to herself, it fell on her long feet when removing the hearth piece from her grotte.

The night began to die down as Camille Bernou de Rochetaillée was at a table with Noemi de Sàrközi of La Grève des Forgerons. They had both been bored. Camille was cradling her jaw in her palm and sighing. She usually gave herself far too many airs, but they were all so graceful that she exuded allure through a mouth that held too many teeth. The women talked of gestures, periods, fashions, crinolines, handkerchiefs to be held in the center. The charming subtle movements of Camille's lips pressed against the mesh of spotted veil on her face. These women were considered the pinnacle of smartness when it came to fashion. They had just finished making fun of Odette Yount for her farthingale pointed lace ruff and pointed stomacher with bombasted sleeves. "It attributes to a wholly Parisian refinement to her appearance."

"Yes, it has a vintage feel, like emptying my chamber pot into the alleyways," Camille responded.

Noemi began to fiddle with her Eton crop as if she had not put enough Brilliantine in. She looked La Garçonne down to her bone. "Did you see Monsieur Childress make an appearance here? He was a stiff brute complaining about his tachycardia. He claims to live with the most fragile of stomachs, a gastric affliction of sorts where he must always pay his tributes if you catch me," Noemi winked as she spoke. "He is rheumaticky and mottled. Did you hear the rumor that he combed his hair over his ears? Either because they had been affected by otitis or he simply cut them off."

Camille was rustling in her seat in a short dress of silver lamé with an astrakhan collar. "There can be no excuse for this bore upon two hours of human life. I am wondering how soon until an expansive, enveloping boredom pours down from the ceiling, smothering all the tables covered with second rate cloth. Hopefully there will be some spark to animate this graveyard. George Lapape's parties have quite a sumptuous concept of riveting but the execution falls short. This is neither."

Noemi sighed as loud as she could, looking for attention. "Ou sont les neiges d'antan. I forgot to mention, I had been furious, I was longing for a rabbit-skin rug in big lush circles of greys and pearls edged with frilles and frufrues of velvet. It cost 1,930 francs. The furrier wouldn't drop the price. He ended up raising it to 1,980. It's unlikely for me to do good work with a furrier," Noemi groaned.

"They are like street urchins over pennies. They might as well stop the sun from rising."

"It's difficult enough to have heaps of money, but it would be a personal hell horns if one had to deny themselves of spending it."

"Remember when the gold franc was seen eye to eye with the silver sterling?" Camille asked.

"Of course. Here we have poor people who were sweating their blood to feed the ambition and pomp of their own grisette. Those slaves of town talk."

"The poor, my dear? They don't exist anymore," Camille proclaimed. "Needlewomen and fishwives wear velvets and dresses of silks when they used to make five pennies an hour. The local slaughterhouse manager just bought a car. There used to be competent and loyal maids-of-all-work, who could be hired for three hundred francs a year with no vacation and seldom a day off, you could tip your cocher four sous and a dinner at La Meurice could be had for one fifty with an additional twenty centimes for Brussels. In fact my gardener lives in the Latin Quarter, in an apartment with enough room for him and his petite amie. Cost of living is low."

Noemi steered the subject toward me. "Have you made Jules' acquaintance yet?"

"Not yet."

"Some would say he is addicted to the pleasure of offending. Jules is a rare man indeed, he has an incredibly challengeable opinion on every subject but never gives it out unless people are asking for it."

"He has said some things very tart, meaning to ruffle some skirts."

"I have noticed though that everyone walks around on their wedding day as if they have peacock feathers stuck to their rears," Noemi shook her head. "Not him though, I heard he reads Voltaire and decided to rescue his lost soul. With him, it's carnival humor gritting its teeth with moral casuistry."

"I'm not sure he is the man to fall headlong in love and repent it for the rest of his short life."

"Nobody, least of all an orphan, enjoys being used as a fulcrum for somebody else's ambitions. Phèdre fears the fading of her charms so she found herself a head start."

Camille shook her head. "One day of happiness and forty years at the end of the table."

Noemi laughed and smacked Camille's wrist with a butterfly-embroidered fan. The oceans of murmurs began to quiet down. The guests telling of all little tittle tattles and witticisms, but there were no longer things to be said. Duchesses whispered, unfertile but loud with shared memories of gardens and villas. My hatreds hidden ulcers eat. I have searched for even a suggestive hint of a parallel among the hundreds of people here now that I could hopefully call my acquaintances and societal equal, but it's been in vain. These are people of varying depths and intricacies of character, but there is no one that can be compared with me. I have gifted myself this blank mind of sand and barrenness, but when combined with rumors, gossip, old wives tales, hazardous turns, and one million thoughts rushing to line up at once, even the my incredible patience and fortitude run dry.

"Japan will never get China, never. China will always fight 'em. It may fall down sometime, even for long, but they get back up. They will drive them back, back to the islands they came from." Solly was sniffing up the snot that came out of his nose between every ten words he spoke. He began to adjust his facial expression to soften his ugly features and appear more presentable than he actually was. "This is the lan of wonderful ants, who burrow they homes in the Earth. I stopped believin' in a heaven the way people imagine it to be. With this I wanna say that there really can't be too much of a difference between up there and down here. I know Heaven down here very well. The Chinese, this mocked and abused nation, they inhabit Heaven down here by themselves. It's the mountains that we base Heaven on. We name it after the mountains. We imagine that only eternal forces can let us in, I think the answer is in the Chinese. It's here somewhere. They've walled off themselves with a wonda of the world and they are so very peaceful. They don't want the world's squabbles. Never does it want or expect things from others, they don't threaten wit war or demans, but states and countries harass them and exploit them. Right up to today, this will be it. The Japanese will find their place in Hell. I do not believe Hell is reserved for my Nigras. I have however believed it certainly isn't barred for Whites neither. I only mention this cuz among the things I believe, one bein' about the height of Heaven, how can we understand anything past the moon because it's all considered part of the Earth and we all need space for ourselves? The Chinese will outlast us and errone else."

"As an anti-militarist, I seek in vain to wish peace but in nature's work, war is in mind and it can be difficult to avoid. I wonder if one day it will become avoidable. The red will always come to the breast of the robin. The valleys haven't changed nor will they, though they shiver faintly from time's reach. Maybe we are to be the same way."

"Amen," Solly said, blowing his nose into his shirt. "May the temper of the body be as the temper of his Parish."

"Uncompromising is the severity of this country at the moment. I too was coming from Nanjing, Solly," I said, leaning forward and offering a handkerchief from my pack. "I had heard the screams. I had seen the flames and avoided it at all costs."

"It's the Devil. It's him for sho'. Cuz there ain't really nuthin' evil in this world, some thins appear warped and unnatural cuz they been badly done in. In orda to be happy in the face of collapse, in all worldly grandeurs, we must go back to the Christian life, subject as we are to it. We must go back to these immutable laws, according to which we undoubtedly shall reap what we sow." Solly began sniffling his way through his words like thick brush. "We will lose along the way, that's the way of thins. To Christ the Savior whose Bleeding Heart by its sacrifice fecundates the Earth's soul. I say give tongue to what he suffered and enjoyed."

"I've been lost to the touch myself," I replied.

"How so?" Solly asked, his eyes bloodshot from the tears.

"Some would say I am a transcendental atheist, if I may say so myself, I'd call it more of an artistic positivist, a lyricist calling against the German sub-theories from on high, unable and unwilling to care for a child in this world and time. God is absent and I simply cannot be cognizant of the immensity of sin."

Solly looked appalled as if he had never heard such words before. "The universe in its darkling manner longs to enter into touch with us, Jules. If they ain't no God, there is somethin' there. Somethin' warm. Heaven is a plain watch and without figures winds and God gave me my identity and in that moment my mami brought me to the font. I just know this." He handed the handkerchief back to me.

"Keep it," I said. "I have failed again and again to untangle the skein of this massive secret. I figure I can open the bones and find nothing. And so, then, it seems an ordinary life enough, to an ordinary person, is an uncomfortable life. That's as it may be, to me it is an empty, damned weariness."

Solly shook his head and looked in the dirt. "Don't say that. I am re-begot! How bored would you be in Heaven, Jules? Your mind is juss havin' its baddies."

"And it has been this way for some time now," I said.

"You've loved though?"

"I thought I did."

He looked up at me with a titled head.

"I've done bad and deserve even worse."

"Well, I gossip on whosa goin' to Hell or not," Solly responded quickly. "This don't guarantee I'm a good man that errbody likes. I'm gentle and smart and I can sing that song about havin' your hiney wiped by a niggermammy in perfect key but God, I do wanna know how anything visible or invisible to the human eye can be transformed by the well-thought mind, good will, and hard work? And that goes for braille text and all objects smallest to biggest or anythin'. There ain't nuthin' to be desired more than to be born and to die within the sound of the church bell that rung for a man's communion and baptism and announced all of life's great moments."

I replied with a noncommittal mutter, unsure if I was even speaking.

"I saw my neighbor peering out from their closed curtains in the middle of June. I saw the shutters move. They certainly were still there."

This particular, unknown wedding guest was prodding her index finger in the direction of the woman she was in conversation with.

"Be quiet and look," the other woman whispered, focused on me and my wife as we made our way upstairs. "This part is very simple: you pick up your dress, you rise from the head table, you thank the guests and then you go upstairs on tiptoe."

"Why on tiptoe?"

"So as not to wake them, my dear."

The women began to titter as the crowd came to a hush. The servants brought out buckets, filling them with the remains of dinner. Whole roast chickens, pheasants, quails, half peeled fruit, they were all pushed off the table into steel buckets. They were going to take the food away and burn it. This waste shocked me—the way people ate. I thought of the hungry poor and women who prowled around and traded services for meals, of children begging for someone to treat them once in their short, miserable lives. I thought about the waste, the French who leave their plates with something that was previously set before them, good manners foreboding them from finishing up to show they were no longer hungry.

We said our goodbyes and made our curtseys as we ascended up the stairs. We made our way to Phèdre's room which reflected the spirit of her parlor. It contained a harp, a portrait of Saint Vincent, and a view of Coppet by moonlight. There were porcelain cherubs which were the work of Florentine artists. The windows were open, the fibers of wicker baskets flicked in the wind though they were not touched. The bedroom was large with canopies, low sofas, satin cushions, and hanging brass lamps with colored glass. The bed was fashioned out of mammoth ebony. Behind a diaphanous, hanging with gold flecks and muted blues, an immense Moorish bowl whose water was heated by a brass boiler of oriental repousse lay dormant. In the clothes cupboard were hundreds of articles of clothing hung like banners arranged by aux nuances les plus tendres. Boucher designed tapestries decorated the walls. I helped untie her corset. She artfully liberated her walnut locks by removing the jeweled comb. Her voice was a slab of concrete:

"Is this real?" she asked. "Is it true that you have possibly ruined everything now? Are you guilty of this?" There were tears in her eyes.

"Of what do you exactly speak?" But of that, I knew. Phèdre, my dearest wife, was much more cunning than I ever could have imagined to be. She knew of my intentions, the unbearable burden that crushed my chest until my heart fell out.

"Could my despair alone not restrain you?" she whimpered. "At least you should reconsider."

"Of–"

She cut me off with her abrasive tone. "If you only knew what I suffer now," the tears had escaped as Phèdre spoke, they ran down her cheeks as she made her way across the room.

"I..."

I stopped speaking as Phèdre picked up a sharp letter opener near the edge of the bed. "Farewell," she said, as she dropped her comb on the bed. She lifted the knife quickly and brought it down as she began to cut into her inner thigh with the letter opener.

I made a lunge for her, but recoiled as she decided to turn it in my direction. I stopped on the carpet and froze.

"For a week now Phèdre, you have been offending me with the most craven and ungodly suspicions pertaining to Lozana and others. I am only committed to you. You are the mother I have never had, you are the everything I have missed in my years."

"It is true when you are gone, I am always torn by the iron fingernails of jealousy. But rest easy, you liar, yet I will love you. Today I have loved you the most, now I drag myself wearily being but the spectral black firs of what you have destroyed."

"Any scandal here would do damage to you and its effect upon your circle and salon would impact you deeply, it may even scar," I said. "This I understand. You would cultivate your hatred toward me, my enemies would find me lacking in gratitude and being churlish but I cannot allow myself to be swept away. The social pages, the gossip columns, all of it made me realize too late that man forfeits his anonymity in favor for courage and recognized talent. I was not ready for this. Phèdre, I do not know if I can do this."

"Why must you forget, Jules, that your feelings were supposed to turn into something magical and innocent," Phèdre cried. "That genius inside you is something else, it is your devil, and it wants to be young forever. There is no doubt your amorality is afraid of my purity because I am pure and only that. I am in some way or another, the right shape, the right size and the right mind to be a wife of whomever I want and with that I chose you."

"I could no more pretend a projectable feeling than swallow absinthe," I blurted out. "I am at a dead end." The pressure had become unbearable as every word left my mouth, my chest bubbled up inside me feeling as if it was filled with cold blood. I knew what I had to do, though it shredded me inside. I had to make sure this decision did not kill what good was left in Paris.

"My heart is running dry with you, Jules. I may become ice overnight." She turned the knife on herself and began to slice into her thigh, drawing the blood onto the blade as she winced. "You were to take care of my feelings," she said. "To preserve my love and hold myself nearest to my own perfections."

"You seem to remember rather well the privilege of confidence that your friends have accorded you but not enough of their weaknesses and miseries which have need of discretion. You call a spade a spade, you prattle on with ease about those you should care for, disposing them rather too easily." I had been becoming increasingly more burdened with each word, to the point of upsetting myself into destruction.

"Does this sound easy to you, Julian?" she asked. "It's not. I am not fussing, though I should be. I can't be your spiritual director for this seminary that awaits us downstairs. They will destroy you if you do not take your leave off the balcony."

Phèdre took the blood on the blade and smeared it in the center of the bed sheets without looking back at me.

It is love she idolizes, love her obsession to be. *You only admire hatred* she tells me, I try to show her that France's breathing, living life is precisely that of darker truths, ugly glories, famous men who deserve to be forgotten. It was me who was to lighten the city's heavy shoulders, who was to disperse the miasma, who was told to hold French spirits as a precious, delicate jewel balanced on the edge of antiquity and ruin and in the midst of all this I was to remain positive. Phèdre put the letter opener away, but not before wiping it clean. She turned to speak:

"There is a god among men and sometimes there inside you too, a child, spoiled and rotten, unwillful and wicked," the tears were flowing as she spoke. "Don't come back until your heart has white hair."

I turned my back to the devil in her diadem and Christ dress of Titiwangsa butterflies, shouldered Sambalpur water lilies, and a carpet of roses. She was on her way to kiss the marbled statue dressed as Hera, throwing flowers in her face.

"You will see an immense field of boulders and rivers, Jules. The city where you were not. Farewell."

I escaped into the summer night, the fireflies splayed about the cedars like glitter in the air.

"The last thing she said befo' she died, there stands the devil at my bed feets to receive my soul when I die? Why? Why she say that?"

"That I am unsure of," I said.

"Is it cuz in these times and in Mobile, people did not make good?" Solly yawned as he spoke. "The night is fresh for sleep, the weather is perfect. You can take rest indoors or out. To your pleasure, good sir. I apologize though, they seem to be plaques of dung errwhere."

I decided to sleep outside and said goodnight to Solly. I took my rest as the moon surveyed with a candle and the stars pointed out the stumbles we sometimes have to face. In the silence of the dark, I could hear Solly whispering himself to sleep. "Sola, Sola, Sola." He began weeping.

My eyes began to shut. Say Goodnight. Goodnight.

Goodnight.

Good.

Night

A face I do not know is forced upon me there.

"We could not print your drawing in gold on white as you asked us to do because the sellers here are very averse to a white binding. It soils too easily. We tried to do a red on gray canvas but it did not come out the way we had expected. We think the blue, gray, and black looks well enough, but one has trouble admiring the engravings. To it, the delicacy of your drawing is lost." A patch of late spring crocuses covered the grass around the art dealer, prompting sad reflections of our aging. "If you can't accept the loss, then frigg off." The art dealer was wearing wide pagoda-like sleeves surrounding himself in hackneyed loadstones. "You are the painter of waist-wasps. You must be coming to Salpêtrière to save them," he proclaimed with thunder. "You are a beggar which must be made to wait and thicken its shell on the side of life's happenings while Time is a Grand Duke on whom all have to wait on patiently before welcoming him when he finally arrives in his opulence. Did you see your headstone? It was ruined by fate, ruined by rich fortune, stuck into a marriage, died in a private cesspool, the Earth, wanting so badly to cover you. Do you want to live to the fin de siècle?"

I hung suspended. I attempted to reply but no words left my mouth. The man continued:

"The old panda fox died before 150 candles. Now the foxes are fin de siècles, studious by day and night. There will be no funereal because there is nothing ever different, nothing ever happens, but there is always an inviolable secrecy as to all that passed in society." The art dealer disappeared before quickly returning. *"They say you must be careful, a simple remark to another artist about their work would be considered impertinent and it is human nature, it is ingrained in us that we compliment and that the appreciation is either ignored or seen as passive-aggressive passes. They said there were stereotyped formulas, what wonder! How interesting a piece! Other artists interpret it as: He won't last long! My God! The anonymous letter is its own genre, Mein Fraulein."*

An old soldier with skinny calves and shredded clothes walked by, he was on the search for pleasure, the feeling of eiderdown between his toes and piles of dry carpet. He was tasting from the danger of the world as associated with a bag of bees and Chos Choches. Solly was there all of a sudden.

"We could juss be nuts and bolts that fettered stained feet," he began to cry in all his lost faith. *"Have you seen my love?"*

"Have you seen my love?"

"Have you–"

"My Love?"

In the morning I awoke, the sun rapidly drank up the last of the night's glistening dew and picked out brilliant hues on the inaccessible crags. Magpies and other birds above on the branch sang:

Cha cha cha cha cha cha
Ken-kwan ken-kwan ken-kwan

Solly was sitting next to me, collecting the

ashes from the fire which had just been burning its last embers. "Lissen," he whispered. "You hear the movement of the Earth under its crust, in the mountains, and under the frost?"

I sat up. "Do I?"

"There are hidden tongues in the trees, there are words found sometimes in the brooks, stories in the stones, and good to be found in errthing," Solly said.

"It's reason to get up in the morning and get right to work," I replied.

"Oh yes," Solly laughed. "But as food without salt is savorless, so is work without play."

"And with that, I should find my way onward."

"I can offer up some ghee and goat's milk before goin' on."

I was getting to my feet now. "No thank you."

"Stay a lil' longer," Solly's voice cracked. "Lay right back down and talk for a while."

"Slow down and rest? With all eternity before me? I think not," I said, stretching out with a gaping yawn. "How do I find my way down to the river?"

Solly looked up at me as I was standing on the other side of the fire pit with my hands in my pockets. "Otha side of the mountain, but you gonna need a boat to cross if you plannin' on crossin', they ain't a bridge for miles and miles."

"I know how to fashion a raft," I lied.

"That ain't good enough, those torrents'll take ya." All I could see was the whites of his eyes as he talked with me, cracked and red.

"I wish you good fortune, Solly," I approached him.

"Spare it, it's an attribute reserved for generals and the Lord." He put his hand out, it was large, cracked, and calloused. "May you whose was sent by papal decree, though driven by impulses, be directed by papal guidance." Solly stood up and shook my hand and he pulled me in tightly to kiss my cheek. I began to walk away as he watched me, standing still in his place. I only made it a few metres before I turned around.

"Solly," I shouted. "Meixiang might still be out there. When the war ends. Go back. Find her."

Solly swallowed and took a deep breath, pointing off into the distance. "The storm will die away and still we will be restless, unwillin', as if the storm was bout to break again. We will think about all that which has disappeared, we will be destroyed by what has been destroyed, what will be new, what will be born again. We fear the future we do not know, Jules, but not witout some type of reasonin' behind it but beyond all, the mind will stay, and will remain the most damaged wit all the destruction. It will judge only itself, it will doubt itself. It will say it's all its fault. What's done can't be un. But God, he who knows no time, can fix time. We as men are the big clock hand of nature, movin' right quick through life. And this is China, where time seems to mean nuthin' and labor hardly more," Solly put his hands in his pockets as he spoke. "Interesting people are loners, Jules, you cannot meet them." He made his way to his shack and pulled the yak-woven tarp to the side. As I went on I could hear Solly singing to himself.

Sen-jo was near, I could feel it as the feasting mist fell upon the lowlands. These Kimmerian Lands, calling for me to tell me I will return from which the mists first lifted from the Earth. They can't be wrong. The sun can be good for some people, not for me. It turns me red like a crimson crack in a brown cloud misting blood. The blossoms of the apricot blow east to west, and I have tried so hard to keep them from falling as ten thousand ripples sent mist over their flowers. They shine so wet and sweet before being beaten to the ground. The mountain mist ransacked the disheveled vermilion clouds celebrating with victories over the doors between Heaven and Earth.

Along some blurred lines, I had arrived at the edge of the world. A step more and I fall off. I do not take a step. I stand on its edge, and I suffer here. Nothing, oh nothing ever in the world can suffer like the traveler all young and alone! There was no path drawn out. The climb down had been treacherous. Rongs were my death. Strange fissures to accompany me by mountains bridged by crazy looking shelves. There near the wall of the mountain were wild clematis which had the most delicate of brown flowers.

I began to run into many rivulets, where the fish were accessible and plenty. The water was thick with sand, a watersmeet had to be nearby. There I had heard what sounded like boiling water and the approach of thunder. Near the swifter torrents, filling up my ears, only to help promote additional fear and warning of the onrush of these stones and small boulders which may come along to break a leg or ankle. Broken poplar trees and pencil cedars strewn along the river only created even more tension. A hawk seemed to have dropped some entrails, some sort of rodent.

Interesting people are loners, you can never meet them.

Phèdre's father once told me that when a man goes to war in decorative armor, he is courageous and heroic. When that man goes to a party and dresses as festive as he can, he is social, an hour man. But if this man happens to suffer from old age, all these things are viewed as acts of loneliness. They are forgotten and ignored until they beg the Lord God to slip them a clean shave or something else. So they go back home and pull their trousers back up and pursue the road to salvation and God. But it comes to them, if they are to wander unloved, why not as well wander there as through nothing? They say out loud, *I would like to live about eight years of judicious debaucheries and then Death. If you cannot provide the eight years, then just Death.* Life is a journey up a hill, that's what they say. Do we always question the journey when on top? Can we not question why the green comes again to the old hills in the spring? No longer can I bear this torturing wrong as detachment becomes part of the pain of belonging.

I was waiting for the realization to hit hard, the more time we spend on this earth, the more we are here to witness the decline and eventual demise of everything we love, forced to abandon the hopes of youth, forced to abandon an energy and vitality we once felt unrestrained. The pragmatism of adulthood would hit like thousands of pounds upon the mind where it once was hidden. I waited for it to hit. With age, the passions pass away, off come the masks, off come the daggers, off come the shoes, each member once banded disappears off the tracks, but onward pulling this carriage was Time. The wheels clicked and didn't stop. One snowflake in the avalanche will always blame the others. Like the sharp tooth of some breathing dragon, a rock broke the surface, brown and half-responsible for the waterfall. I try to find an answer to my problems. I find one answer but I think it's not enough so I try and find another answer. Now I have two, but I think I need more than that so I try again; then I have three. Not enough, I go at it again harder and faster. I go to theories and philosophies and religion, it is not enough but that's okay for God cannot commit suicide, for his is an eternal existence, poor bastard.

The great tit with its yellow waist coat and black shirt was coming out of the sunlight, onto a rock, and cocked its head at me. Her eye was glassy and bright. She watched me move through the patches of boulders with one eye then twitched. And it would be the other glassy eye. The pump of her chest as fast as my pulse. As I moved toward her, she quit swapping eyes and watched with the one until I got too close and she flew off.

Erat hora. But I could not tell my one friend exactly what I was feeling. I left there and I couldn't tell him. With his peacefullest words and meanings, I treated him like Apollo as I transformed into a laurel tree. His tears did drown me out, and that was my fault and now the year will be lost on me. But still, there I felt a convulsion and a melting within me. And that is how I knew time should drag with me, both as waste. There is no more space left to smell the sudden rain, to think back of Phèdre, Campden Hills, everything I left behind in Paris. The dog carts, the smell of fresh bakeries, reading Leibniz, falling in love and smelling the dinner cooking, Anna la bonne, le philosophie du sourier, hatpin-ducking gentleman, idle and cloistered young girls, Angora cats on leashes being walked in shady parks—people being their best. The sky may be the same everywhere we go, but it's what's underneath it. The past exists in tatters and fragments and we must find a way to represent it as is.

I arrived at my Acheron to be ferried. I believe it was Ch'u-t'ang. The air felt balmy as I patched my way through little stunted white irises chasing out the choughs in a flurry of yellow. I stood still for a moment and felt my breath escape me and welcome it in. Every part of me that wanted to turn toward the light would then drink deep of the lees of death. My garbled existence partakes in both, wandering to one side not before it floats about between the two. With this feeling, the world reveals goosesteps resounding in the darkness, maybe breathtaking will be my leave, my departure is a clue to that. Time and the last melancholy weep, they carry a feeling which cannot be evoked by any other arrangement of shapes, sounds, colors, and noises. Wilst'ou swim in a river strip through an aeon of nothingness? When the raft breaks and the waters rush over me, shores will gradually fade, and I will be lost in the turn of the hills. Only the evening sun and its warmth over the water remain. At night, when the town belongs to its own shadows, I will come here to sit between the boulevards. I will talk to friends of the past, I will go over memories and new thoughts with the night-wanderers while the early-morning workers will eventually pass by, I will always have the last word. But that word, alas, no one will hear.

Thomas Hrycyk is currently a candidate for an MFA at Queens University of Charlotte and has worked for multiple literary publications including *Fifth Wednesday Journal*. He was born in Chicago and holds a B.A. in English and Philosophy from DePaul University. He recently moved to Nashville and works as an educator at Tennessee State University.

www.ingramcontent.com/pod-product-compliance
Lightning Source LLC
Chambersburg PA
CBHW070521130626
46555CB00003B/1297